Remake

Remake

CONNIE WILLIS

BANTAM BOOKS

NEW YORK   TORONTO   LONDON   SYDNEY   AUCKLAND

REMAKE

A Bantam Book / February 1995

SPECTRA and the portrayal of a boxed ''s'' are trademarks of Bantam Books, a division of Bantam
Doubleday Dell Publishing, Inc.

BOOK DESIGN BY GLEN M. EDELSTEIN

Library of Congress Cataloging-in-Publication Data

Willis, Connie.
    Remake / Connie Willis.
        p.   cm.
    ISBN 0-553-37437-0
    I. Title.
    PS3573.I45652R46   1995
    813'.54—dc20   94-28940
                                                                            CIP

Published simultaneously in the United States and Canada

Bantam Books are published by Bantam Books, a division of Bantam Doubleday Dell Publishing
Group, Inc. Its trademark, consisting of the words ''Bantam Books'' and the portrayal of a
rooster, is Registered in U.S. Patent and Trademark Office and in other countries. Marca
Registrada. Bantam Books, 1540 Broadway, New York, New York 10036.

PRINTED IN THE UNITED STATES OF AMERICA
CWO   0 9 8 7 6 5 4 3 2 1

To Fred Astaire

ACKNOWLEDGMENTS

Special thanks to Scott Kippen and Sheryl Beck
and all the rest of the UNC Sigma Tau Deltans

and to

my daughter Cordelia and her statistics classes

and to

my secretary Laura Norton

all of whom
helped come up with chase scenes, tears, happy endings,
and all the other movie references

"Not much is impossible."

> —Steve Williams
> Industrial Light and Magic

"The girl seems to have talent but the boy can do nothing."

> —Vaudeville booking report
> on Fred Astaire

Remake

HOUSE LIGHTS DOWN

Before Titles

I SAW HER AGAIN TONIGHT. I WASN'T LOOKING for her. It was an early Spielberg liveaction, *Indiana Jones and the Temple of Doom,* a cross between a shoot-'em-up and a VR ride and the last place you'd expect tap shoes, and it was too late. The musical had kicked off, as Michael Caine so eloquently put it, in 1965.

This liveaction was made in '84, at the very beginning of the computer graphics revolution, and it had a few CG sections: digitized Thugees being thrown off a cliff and a pathetically clunky morph of a heart being torn out. It also had a Ford Tri-Motor plane, which was what I was looking for when I found her.

I needed the Tri-Motor for the big good-bye scene at the

Connie Willis

airport, so I'd accessed Heada, who knows everything, and she'd said she thought there was one in one of the liveaction Spielbergs, the second Indy maybe. "It's close to the end."

"How close?"

"Fifty frames. Or maybe it's in the third one. No, that's a dirigible. The second one. How's the remake coming, Tom?"

Almost done, I thought. Three years off the AS's and still sober.

"The remake's stuck on the big farewell scene," I said, "which is why I need the plane. So what do you know, Heada? What's the latest gossip? Who's ILMGM being taken over by this month?"

"Fox-Mitsubishi," she said promptly. "Mayer's frantic. And the word is Universal's head exec is on the way out. Too many addictive substances."

"How about you?" I said. "Are you still off the AS's? Still assistant producer?"

"Still playing Melanie Griffith," she said. "Does the plane have to be color?"

"No. I've got a colorization program. Why?"

"I think there's one in *Casablanca*."

"No, there's not," I said. "That's a two-engine Lockheed."

She said, "Tom, I talked to a set director last week who was on his way to China to do stock shots."

I knew where this was leading. I said, "I'll check the Spielberg. Thanks," and signed off before she could say anything else.

The Ford Tri-Motor wasn't at the end, or in the middle, which had one of the worst mattes I'd ever seen. I worked my way back through it at 48 per, thinking it would have been easier to do a scratch construct, and finally found the plane almost at the beginning. It was pretty good—there were close-ups of the door and the cockpit, and a nice medium shot of it taking off. I went back a few frames, trying to see if there was a close-up of the propellers, and then said, "Frame 1-001," in case there was something at the very beginning.

Trademark Spielberg morph of the old Paramount Studios mountain into opening shot, this time of a man-sized silver gong. Cue music. Red smoke. Credits. And there she was, in a chorus line, wearing silver tap shoes and a silver-sequined leotard with tuxedo lapels. Her face was made up thirties style— red lips, Harlow eyebrows—and her hair was platinum blonde.

It caught me off guard. I'd already searched the eighties, looking in everything from *Chorus Line* to *Footloose*, and not found any sign of her.

I said, "Freeze!" and then "Enhance right half," and leaned forward to look at the enlarged image to make sure, as if I hadn't already been sure the instant I saw her.

"Full screen," I said, "forward realtime," and watched the rest of the number. It wasn't much—four lines of blondes in sequined top hats and ribboned tap shoes doing a simple chorus routine that could have been lifted from *42nd Street,* and was about as good. There must not have been any dancing teachers around in the eighties either.

The steps were simple, mostly trenches and traveling steps, and I thought it had probably been one of the very first ones Alis did. She had been this good when I saw her practicing in the film hist classroom. And it was too Berkeleyesque. Near the end of the number it went to angles and a pan shot of red scarves being pulled out of tuxedo pockets, and Alis disappeared. The Digimatte couldn't have matched that many switching shots, and I doubted if Alis had even tried. She had never had any patience with Busby Berkeley.

"It isn't dancing," she'd said, watching the kaleidoscope scene in *Dames* that first night in my room.

"I thought he was famous for his choreography," I'd said.

"He is, but he shouldn't be. It's all camera angles and stage sets. Fred Astaire always insisted his dances be shot full-length and one continuous take."

"Frame ten," I said so I wouldn't have to put up with the mountain morph again, and started through the routine again. "Freeze."

The screen froze her in midkick, her foot in the silver tap shoe extended the way Madame Dilyovska of Meadowville had taught her, her arms outstretched. She was supposed to be smiling, but she wasn't. She had a look of intentness, of careful concentration under the scarlet lipstick, the penciled brows, the look she had worn that first night, watching Ginger Rogers and Fred Astaire on the freescreen.

"Freeze," I said again, even though the image hadn't moved, and sat there for a long time, thinking about Fred Astaire and looking at her face, that face I had seen under endless wigs, in endless makeups, that face I would have known anywhere.

TITLE UP

*Opening Credits
and Dissolve to
Pan Shot of Party Scene*

MOVIE CLICHE #14: The Party. Disjointed snatches of bizarre conversation, excessive AS consumption, assorted outrageous behavior.

SEE: *Notorious, Greed, The Graduate, Risky Business, Breakfast at Tiffany's, Dance, Fools, Dance, The Party*.

S HE WAS BORN THE YEAR FRED ASTAIRE DIED. Hedda told me that the first time I met Alis. It was at one of the dorm parties the studios sponsor. There's one every week, ostensibly to show off their latest CG innovations and try to tempt hackate film-school seniors into a life of digitizing and indentured servitude, really so their execs can score some chooch (of which there is never enough) and some popsy (of which there is plenty, all of it in white halter dresses and platinum hair). Hollywood at its finest, which is why I stay away, but this one was being sponsored by ILMGM, and Mayer had promised me he'd be there.

Connie Willis

I'd been doing a paste-up for him, digitizing his studio exec boss's popsy into a River Phoenix movie. I wanted to give Mayer the opdisk and get paid before the boss found a new face. I'd already done the paste-up twice and fed in the feedback bypasses three times because he'd switched girlfriends, and this last time the new face had insisted on a scene *with* River Phoenix, which meant I'd had to watch every River Phoenix movie ever made, of which there are a lot—he was one of the first actors copyrighted. I wanted to get the money before Mayer's boss changed partners again. The money and some AS's.

The party was crammed into the dorm lounge, like always—freshies and faces and hackates and hangers-on. The usual suspects. There was a big fibe-op freescreen in the middle of the room. I glanced up at it, hoping to God it wasn't the new River Phoenix movie, and was surprised to see Fred Astaire and Ginger Rogers, dancing up a flight of stairs. Fred was wearing tails, and Ginger was in a white dress that flared into black at the hem. I couldn't hear the music over the party din, but it looked like the Continental.

I couldn't see Mayer. There was a guy in an ILMGM baseball cap and a beard—the hackates' uniform—standing under the freescreen with a remote, holding forth to a couple of CG majors. I scanned the crowd, looking for suits and/or somebody I knew who'd give me some chooch.

"Hi," one of the faces said breathily. She had platinum hair, a white halter dress, and a beauty mark, and she was very splatted. Her eyes weren't focusing at all.

"Hi," I said, still scanning the crowd. "And who are you supposed to be? Jean Harlow?"

"Who?" she said, and I wanted to believe that that was because of whatever AS she was doing, but it probably wasn't. Ah, Hollywood, where everybody wants to be in the movies and nobody's ever bothered to watch one.

"Jeanne Eagles?" I said. "Carole Lombard? Kim Basinger?"

"*No,*" she said, trying to focus. "Marilyn Monroe. Are you a studio exec?"

"Depends. Do you have any chooch?"

"No," she said sadly. "All gone."

"Then I'm not a studio exec," I said. I could see an exec, though, over by the stairs, talking to another Marilyn. The Marilyn was wearing a white halter dress just like the one I was talking to had on.

I've never understood why the faces, who have nothing to sell but an original personality, an original face, all try to look like somebody else. But I guess it makes sense. Why should they be different from everybody else in Hollywood, which has always been in love with sequels and imitations and remakes?

"Are you in the movies?" my Marilyn persisted.

"Nobody's in the movies," I said, and started toward the studio exec through the crush.

It was harder work than hauling the *African Queen* through the reeds. I edged my way between a group of faces talking about a rumor that Columbia Tri-Star was hiring warmbodies, and then a couple of geekates in data helmets at some other party altogether, and over to the stairs.

I couldn't tell it wasn't Mayer till I got close enough to hear the exec's voice—studio execs are as bad as Marilyns. They all look alike. And have the same line.

" . . . looking for a face for my new project," he was saying. The new project was a remake of *Back to the Future* starring, natch, River Phoenix. "It's a perfect time to rerelease," he said, leaning down the Marilyn's halter top. "They say we're *this* close"—he held his thumb and forefinger together, almost touching—"to getting the real thing."

"The real thing?" the Marilyn said, in a fair imitation of Marilyn Monroe's breathy voice. She looked more like her than mine had, though she was a little thick in the waist. But the faces don't worry about that as much as they used to. A few extra pounds can be didged out. Or in. "You mean time travel?"

"I mean time travel. Only it won't be in a DeLorean. It'll be in a time machine that looks like the skids. We've already come up with the graphics. The only thing we don't have is an actress to play opposite River. The director wanted to go with Michelle Pfeiffer or Lana Turner, but I told him I think we should go with an unknown. Somebody with a new face, somebody special. You interested in being in the movies?"

I'd heard this line before. In *Stage Door*. 1937.

I waded back into the party and over to the freescreen, where the baseball-cap-and-beard was holding forth to some freshies. " . . . programmed for any shots you want. Dolly shots, split-screens, pans. Say you want a close-up of this guy." He pointed up at the screen with the remote.

"Fred Astaire," I said. "That guy is Fred Astaire."

"You punch in 'close-up'—"

Fred Astaire's face filled the screen, smiling.

"This is ILMGM's new edit program," the baseball cap said to me. "It picks angles, combines shots, makes cuts. All you need is a full-length base shot to work from, like this one." He hit a button on the remote, and a full-length shot of Fred and Ginger replaced Fred's face. "Full-length shots are hard to come by. I had to go all the way back to the b-and-w's to find anything long enough, but we're working on that."

He hit another button, and we were treated to a view of Fred's mouth, and then his hand. "You can do any edit program you want," Baseball Cap said, watching the screen. Fred's mouth again, the white carnation in his lapel, his hand. "This one takes the base shot and edits it using the shot sequence of the opening scene from *Citizen Kane*."

A medium-shot of Ginger, and then of the carnation. I wondered which one was supposed to be Rosebud.

"It's all preprogrammed," Baseball Cap said. "You don't have to do a thing. It does everything."

"Does it know where Mayer is?" I asked.

"He *was* here," he said, looking vaguely around, and then back at the screen, where Fred was going through his paces. "It can extrapolate long shots, aerials, two-shots."

"Have it extrapolate somebody who knows where Mayer is," I said, and went back over the side and into the water. The party was getting steadily more crowded. The only ones with any room at all to move were Fred and Ginger, swirling up and down the staircase.

The exec I'd seen before was in the middle of the room, pitching to the same Marilyn, or a different one. Maybe he knew where Mayer was. I started toward him, and then spotted Hedda in a pink strapless sheath and diamond bracelets. *Gentlemen Prefer Blondes.*

Hedda knows everything, all the news, all the gossip. If anybody knew where Mayer was, it'd be Hedda. I waded my way over to her, past the exec, who was explaining time travel to the Marilyn. "It's the same principle as the skids," he said. "The Casimir effect. The randomized electrons in the walls create a negative-matter region that produces an overlap interval."

He must have been a hackate before he morphed into an exec.

"The Casimir effect lets you overlap space to get from one skids station to another, and the same thing's theoretically possible for getting from one parallel timefeed to another. I've got an opdisk that explains it all," he said, running his hand down her haltered neck. "How about if we go up to your room and take a look at it?"

I squeezed past him, hoping I wouldn't come up covered with leeches, and hauled myself out next to Hedda. "Mayer here?" I asked.

"Nope," she said, her platinum head bent over an assortment of cubes and capsules in her pink-gloved hand. "He was here for a few minutes, but he left with one of the freshies. And when the party started there was a guy from Disney nosing around. The word is Disney's scouting a takeover of ILMGM.''

Another reason to get paid now. ''Did Mayer say if he was coming back?''

She shook her head, still deep in her study of the pharmacy.

''Any chooch in there?'' I said.

''I think these are,'' she said, handing me two purple-and-white capsules. ''A face gave me this stuff, and he told me which was which, but I can't remember. I'm pretty sure those are the chooch. I took some. I can let you know in a minute.''

''Great,'' I said, wishing I could take them now. Mayer's leaving with a freshie might mean he was pimping again, which meant another paste-up. ''What's the word on Mayer's boss? His new girlfriend dump him yet?''

She looked instantly interested. ''Not that I know of. Why? Did you hear something?''

''No.'' And if Hedda hadn't either, it hadn't happened. So Mayer'd just taken the freshie up to her dorm room for a quick pop or a quicker line or two of flake, and he'd be back in a few minutes, and I might actually get paid.

I grabbed a paper cup from a Marilyn swaying past and downed the capsules.

''So, Hedda,'' I said, since talking to her was better than to the baseball cap or the time-travel exec, ''what other gossip you putting in your column this week?''

''Column?'' she said, looking blank. ''You always call me Hedda. Why? Is she a movie star?''

Connie Willis

"Gossip columnist," I said. "Knew everything that was going on in Hollywood. Like you. So what is? Going on?"

"Viamount's got a new automatic foley program," she said promptly. "ILMGM's getting ready to file copyrights on Fred Astaire *and* Sean Connery, who finally died. And the word is Pinewood's hiring warmbodies for the new *Batman* sequel. And Warner's——" She stopped in midword and frowned down at her hand.

"What's the matter?"

"I don't think it's chooch. I'm getting a funny . . . " She peered at her hand. "Maybe the yellow ones were the chooch." She fished through her hand. "This feels more like ice."

"Who gave them to you?" I said. "The Disney guy?"

"No. This guy I know. A face."

"What does he look like?" I asked. Stupid question. There are only two varieties: James Dean and River Phoenix. "Is he here?"

She shook her head. "He gave them to me because he was leaving. He said he wouldn't need them anymore, and besides, he'd get arrested in China for having them."

"China?"

"He said they've got a liveaction studio there, and they're hiring stunt doubles and warmbodies for their propaganda films."

And I'd thought doing paste-ups for Mayer was the worst job in the world.

"Maybe it's redline," she said, poking at the capsules. "I hope not. Redline always makes me look like shit the next day."

"Instead of like Marilyn Monroe," I said, looking around the room for Mayer. He still wasn't back. The time-travel exec was edging toward the door with a Marilyn. The data-helmet geekates were laughing and snatching at air, obviously at a much better party than this one. Fred and Ginge were demonstrating another editing program. Rapid-fire cuts of Ginger, the ballroom curtains, Ginger's mouth, the curtains. It must be the shower scene from *Psycho*.

The program ended and Fred reached for Ginger's outstretched hand, her black-edged skirt flaring with momentum, and spun her into his arms. The edges of the freescreen started going to soft-focus. I looked over at the stairs. They were blurring, too.

"Shit, this isn't redline," I said. "It's klieg."

"It is?" she said, sniffing at it.

It is, I thought disgustedly, and what was I supposed to do now? Flashing on klieg wasn't any way to do a meeting with a sleaze like Mayer, and the damned stuff isn't good for anything else. No rush, no halluces, not even a buzz. Just blurred vision and then a flash of indelible reality. "Shit," I said again.

"If it is klieg," Hedda said, stirring it around with her gloved finger, "we can at least have some great sex."

"I don't need klieg for that," I said, but I started looking around the room for somebody to pop. Hedda was right. Flashing during sex made for an unforgettable orgasm. Literally. I scanned the Marilyns. I could do the exec's casting couch number on one of the freshies, but there was no way to tell how long that would take, and it felt like I only had a few minutes.

The Marilyn I'd talked to before was over by the freescreen listening to the studio exec's time-travel spiel.

I looked over at the door. A girl was standing in the doorway, gazing tentatively around at the party as if she were looking for somebody. She had curly light brown hair, pulled back at the sides. The doorway behind her was dark, but there had to be light coming from somewhere because her hair shone like it was backlit.

"Of all the gin joints in all the world . . . " I said.

"Joint?" Hedda said, deep in her pill assortment. "I thought you said it was klieg." She sniffed it.

The girl had to be a face, she was too pretty not to be, but the hair was wrong, and so was the costume, which wasn't a halter dress and wasn't white. It was black, with a green fitted weskit, and she was wearing short green gloves. Deanna Durbin? No, the hair was the wrong color. And it was tied back with a green hair ribbon. Shirley Temple?

"Who's that?" I muttered.

"Who?" Hedda licked her gloved finger and rubbed it in the powder the pills had left on her glove.

"The face over there," I said, pointing. She had moved out of the doorway, over against the wall, but her hair was still catching the light, making a halo of her light brown hair.

Hedda sucked the powder off her glove. "Alice," she said.

Alice who? Alice Faye? No, Alice Faye'd been a platinum blonde, like everybody else in Hollywood. And she wasn't given to hair ribbons. Charlotte Henry in *Alice in Wonderland*?

Whoever the girl had been looking for—the White Rabbit, probably—she'd given up on finding him, and was watching the freescreen. On it, Fred and Ginger were dancing around each other without touching, their eyes locked.

"Alice who?" I said.

Hedda was frowning at her finger. "Huh?"

"Who's she supposed to be?" I said. "Alice Faye? Alice Adams? *Alice Doesn't Live Here Anymore?*"

The girl had moved away from the wall, her eyes still on the screen, and was heading toward the baseball cap. He leaped forward, thrilled to have a new audience, and started into his spiel, but she wasn't listening to him. She was watching Fred and Ginge, her head tilted up toward the screen, her hair catching the light from the fibe-op feed.

"I don't think any of this stuff is what he told me," Hedda said, licking her finger again. "It's her name."

"What?"

"Alice," she said. "A-l-i-s. It's her name. She's a freshie. Film hist major. From Illinois."

Well, that explained the hair ribbon, though not the rest of the getup. It wasn't Alice Adams. The gloves were 1950s, not thirties, and her face wasn't angular enough to be trying for Katharine Hepburn. "Who's she supposed to be?"

"I wonder which one of these is ice," Hedda said, poking around in her hand again. "It's supposed to make the flash go away faster. She wants to dance in the movies."

"I think you've had enough pill potluck," I said, reaching for her hand.

She squeezed it shut, protecting the pills. "No, really. She's a dancer."

I looked at her, wondering how many unmarked pills she'd taken before I got here.

"She was born the year Fred Astaire died," she said, gesturing with her closed fist. "She saw him on the fibe-op feed and decided to come to Hollywood to dance in the movies."

"*What* movies?" I said.

She shrugged, intent on her hand again.

I looked over at the girl. She was still watching the screen, her face intent. "Ruby Keeler," I said.

"Huh?" Hedda said.

"The plucky little dancer in *42nd Street* who wants to be a star." Only she was about twenty years too late. But just in time for a little popsy, and if she was wide-eyed enough to believe she could make it in the movies, it ought to be a piece of cake getting her up to my room.

I shouldn't have to explain time travel to her, like the exec. He was talking earnestly to a Marilyn wearing black fringe and holding a ukelele. *Some Like It Hot.*

"See, you're turning me down in this timefeed," he was saying, "but in a parallel timefeed we're already popping." He leaned closer. "There are hundreds of thousands of parallel timefeeds. Who *knows* what we're doing in some of them?"

"What if I'm turning you down in all of them?" the Marilyn said.

I squeezed past her fringe, thinking she might work out if

Ruby didn't, and started through the crowd toward the screen.

"Don't!" Hedda said loudly.

At least half the room turned to look at her.

"Don't what?" I said, coming back to her. She was looking past me at Alis, and her face had the bleak, slightly dazed look klieg produces.

"You just flashed, didn't you?" I said. "I told you it was klieg. And that means I'll be doing the same thing shortly, so if you'll excuse me—"

She took hold of my arm. "I don't think you should—" she said, still looking at Alis. "She won't . . . " She was looking worriedly at me. Mildred Natwick in *She Wore a Yellow Ribbon,* telling John Wayne to be careful.

"Won't what? Give me a pop? You wanta bet?"

"No," she said, shaking her head like she was trying to clear it. "You . . . she knows what she wants."

"So do I. And thanks to your Russian-roulette approach to pharmaceuticals, it promises to be an unforgettable experience. If I can get Ruby up to my room in the next ten minutes. Now, if there are no further objections . . . " I said, and started past her.

She started to put out her hand, like she was going to grab my sleeve, and then let it drop.

The exec was talking about negative-matter regions. I went around him and over to the screen, where Alis was looking up at Fred's face, the staircase, Ginger's black-edged skirt, Fred's hand.

She was as pretty in close-up as she had been in the establishing shot. Her caught-back hair was picking up the flickering light from the screen and her face had an intent, focused look.

"They shouldn't do that," she said.

"What? Show a movie?" I said. " 'You've got to show a movie at a party. It's a Hollywood law.' "

She turned and smiled delightedly at me. "I know that line. It's from *Singin' in the Rain*," she said, pleased. "I didn't mean the movie. It's them editing it like that." She looked back up at the screen. Or down. It was doing an aerial now, and all you could see were the tops of Fred and Ginger's heads.

"I take it you don't like Vincent's edit program?" I said.

"Vincent?"

I nodded toward the baseball cap, who was off in a corner doing a line of illy. "Doesn't he remind you of Vincent Price in *House of Wax*?"

The edit program was back to quick cuts—the steps, Fred's face, close-up of a step. The baby carriage scene from *Potemkin*.

"In more ways than one," I said.

"Fred Astaire always insisted they shoot his dances in full-length shot and a continuous take," she said without taking her eyes off the screen. "He said it's the only way to film dancing."

"He did, huh? No wonder I like the original better." I looked at her. "I've got it up in my room."

And that made her turn away from Ginger's flashingly cut feet, shoulder, hair, and look at me. It was the same intent, focused look she had had watching the screen, and I felt the edges start to blur.

"No cuts, no camera angles," I said rapidly. "Nothing preprogrammed. Full-length and continuous take. Want to come up and take a look?''

She looked back at the freescreen. Fred's chest, his face, his knees. ''Yes,'' she said. ''You've got the real movie? Not colorized or anything?''

''The real thing,'' I said, and led her up the stairs.

RUBY KEELER: [*Nervously*] I've never been in a man's apartment before.

ADOLPHE MENJOU: [*Pouring champagne*] You've never been in Hollywood before. [*Handing her glass*] Here, my dear, this will relax you.

RUBY KEELER: [*Hovering near door*] You said you had a screen test application up here. Shouldn't I fill it out?

ADOLPHE MENJOU: [*Turning down lights*] Later, my dear, after we've had a chance to get to know each other.

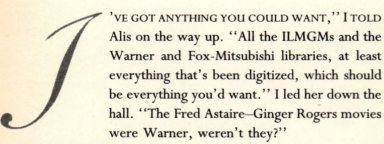

'VE GOT ANYTHING YOU COULD WANT," I TOLD Alis on the way up. "All the ILMGMs and the Warner and Fox-Mitsubishi libraries, at least everything that's been digitized, which should be everything you'd want." I led her down the hall. "The Fred Astaire–Ginger Rogers movies were Warner, weren't they?"

"RKO," she said.

"Same thing." I keyed the door. "Here we are," I said, and opened it onto my room.

She took a trusting step inside and then stopped at the sight of the arrays covering three walls with their mirrored screens. "I thought you said you were a student," she said.

Now was not the time to tell her I hadn't been to class in over a semester. "I am," I said, leaning past her so she'd step forward into the room, and picking up a shirt. "Clothes all over the floor, bed's not made." I lobbed the shirt into the corner. "*Andy Hardy Goes to College.*"

She was looking at the digitizer and the fibe-op feed hookup. "I thought only the studios had Crays."

"I do work for them to help pay for tuition," I said. And keep me in chooch.

"What kind of work?" she said, looking up at her own face's reflection in the silvered screens, and now was not the time to tell her I specialized in procuring popsy for studio execs either.

"Remakes," I said. I smoothed out the blankets. "Sit down."

She perched on the edge of the bed, knees together.

"Okay," I said, sitting down at the comp. I asked for the Warner library menu. "The Continental's in *Top Hat,* isn't it?"

"*The Gay Divorcee,*" she said. "Near the end."

"Main screen, end frame and back at 96," I said. Fred and Ginge leaped onto the screen and up over a table. "Rew at 96 frames per sec," and they jumped down off the table and back through breakfast to the ballroom.

I rew'd to the beginning of the number and let it go. "Do you want sound?" I said.

She shook her head, her face already intent on the screen, and maybe this hadn't been such a great idea. She leaned forward, and the same concentrated look she'd had downstairs came into her face, as if she were trying to memorize the steps. I might as well not have been in the room, which hadn't exactly been the idea in bringing her up here.

"Menu," I said. "Fred Astaire and Ginger Rogers movies." The menu came up. "Aux screen one, *Swingtime*," I said. There was usually a big dance finale in these things, wasn't there? "End frame and back at 96."

There was. On the top left-hand screen, Fred in tails spun Ginge in a silver dress. "Frame 102-044," I said, reading the code at the bottom. "Forward realtime to end and repeat. Continuous loop. Screen two, *Follow the Fleet*, screen three, *Top Hat*, screen four, *Carefree*. End frame and back at 96."

I started continuous loops on them and went through the rest of the Fred and Ginger list, filling most of the left-hand array with their dancing: turning, tapping, twirling, Fred in tails, sailor's uniform, riding tweeds, Ginger in long, slinky dresses that flared out below the knee in a froth of feathers and fur and glitter. Waltzing, tapping, gliding through the Carioca, the Yam, the Piccolino. And all of them full-length. All of them without cuts.

Alis was staring at the screens. The careful, intent look was gone, and she was smiling delightedly.

"Anything else?"

"*Shall We Dance,*" she said. "The title number. Frame 87-1309."

I set it running on the bottom row. Fred in meticulous tails, dancing with a chorus of blondes in black satin and veils. They all held up masks of Ginger Rogers's face, and they put them up in front of their faces and flirted away from Fred, their masks as stiff as faces'.

"Any other movies?" I said, calling up the menu again. "Plenty of screens left. How about *An American in Paris?*"

"I don't like Gene Kelly," she said.

"Okay," I said, surprised. "How about *Meet Me in St. Louis?*"

"There isn't any dancing in it except the 'Under the Banyan Tree' number with Margaret O'Brien. It's because of Judy Garland. She was a terrible dancer."

"Okay," I said, even more surprised. "*Singin' in the Rain?* No, wait, you don't like Gene Kelly."

"The 'Good Mornin' ' number's okay."

I found it, Gene Kelly with Debbie Reynolds and Donald O'Connor, tapping up steps and over furniture in wild exuberance. Okay.

I scanned the menu for movies that didn't have Gene Kelly or Judy Garland in them. "*Good News?*"

" 'The Varsity Drag,' " she said, nodding. "It's right at the end. Do you have *Seven Brides for Seven Brothers?*"

"Sure. Which number?"

"The barnraising," she said. "Frame 27-986."

I called it up. I looked for something with Ruby Keeler in it. "*42nd Street?*"

She shook her head. "It's a Busby Berkeley. There's no dancing in it except for one background shot of a rehearsal and about sixteen bars in the 'Pettin' in the Park' number. There's never any dancing in Busby Berkeleys. Do you have *On the Town*?"

"I thought you didn't like Gene Kelly."

"Ann Miller," she said. "The 'Prehistoric Man' number. Frame 28-650. She's technically pretty good when she sticks to tap."

I don't know why I was so surprised or what I'd expected. Starstruck adoration, I guess. Ruby Keeler gushing, "Gosh, Mr. Ziegfeld, a part in your show! That'd be wonderful!" Or maybe Judy Garland, gazing longingly at the photo of Clark Gable in *Broadway Melody of 1938*. But she didn't like Judy, and she'd dismissed Gene Kelly as airily as if he was an auditioning chorus girl in a Busby Berkeley. Who she didn't like either.

I filled out the array with Fred Astaire, who she *did* like, though none of his color movies were as good as the b-and-w's, and neither were his partners. Most of them just hung on while he swung them around, or struck a pose and let him dance circles, literally, around them.

Alis wasn't watching them. She'd gone back to the center screen and was watching Fred, full-length, swirling Ginger weightlessly across the floor.

"So that's what you want to do," I said, pointing. "Dance the Continental?"

She shook her head. "I'm not good enough yet. I only know a few routines. I could do that," she said, pointing at the Varsity

Drag, and then at the cowboy number from *Girl Crazy*. "And maybe that. Chorus, not lead."

And that wasn't what I expected either. The one thing the faces have in common under their Marilyn beauty marks is the unshakeable belief they've got what it takes to be a star. Most of them don't—they can't act or show emotion, can't even do a reasonable imitation of Norma Jean's breathy voice and sexy vulnerability—but they all think the only thing standing between them and stardom is bad luck, not talent. I'd never heard any of them say, "I'm not good enough."

"I'm going to need to find a dancing teacher," Alis was saying. "You don't know of one, do you?"

In Hollywood? She was as likely to find one as she was to run into Fred Astaire. Less likely.

And what if she *was* smart enough to know how good she was? What if she'd studied the movies and criticized them? None of it was going to bring back musicals. None of it was going to make ILMGM start shooting liveactions again.

I looked up at the arrays. On the bottom row Fred was trying to find the real Ginger in among the masks. On the third screen, top row, he was trying to talk her into a pop—she twirled away from him, he advanced, she returned, he bent toward her, she leaned languorously away.

All of which I'd better get on with or I was going to flash with Alis still sitting there on the edge of the bed, clothes on and knees together.

I asked for sound on Screen Three and sat down next to Alis on the bed. "I think you're good enough," I said.

She glanced at me, confused, and then realized I was picking up on her "I'm not good enough" line. "You haven't seen me dance," she said.

"I wasn't talking about dancing," I said, and bent forward to kiss her.

The center screen flashed white. "Message," it said. "From Heada Hopper." She'd spelled Hedda with an "a." I wondered if Hedda'd had another revelatory flash and was interrupting to tell it to me.

"Message override," I said, and stood up to clear the screen, but it was too late. The message was already on the screen.

"Mayer's here," it read. "Shall I send him up? Heada."

The last thing I wanted was Mayer up here. I'd have to make a copy of the paste-up and take it down to him. "River Phoenix file," I said to the computer, and shoved in a blank opdisk. "*Where the Boys Are*. Record remake."

The dancing screens went blank, and Alis stood up. "Should I go?" she said.

"No!" I said, rummaging for a remote. The comp spit out the disk, and I snatched it up. "Stay here. I'll be right back. I've just got to give this to a guy."

I handed her the remote. "Here. Hit *M* for Menu, and ask for whatever you want. If the movie you want isn't on ILMGM, you can call up the other libraries by hitting File. I'll be back before the Continental's over. Promise."

I started out the door. I wanted to shut the door to keep her there, but it looked more like I'd be right back if I left it open. "Don't leave," I said, and tore downstairs.

Heada was waiting for me at the foot of the stairs. "Sorry," she said. "Were you popping her?"

"Thanks to you, no," I said, scanning the room for Mayer. The room had gotten even more crowded since Alis and I left. So had the screen—a dozen Fred and Gingers were running split-screen circles around each other.

"I wouldn't have interrupted you," Heada said, "but you asked before if Mayer was here."

"It's okay," I said. "Where is he?"

"Over there." She pointed in the direction of the Freds and Gingers. Mayer was under them, listening to Vincent explain his edit program and twitching from too much chooch. "He said he wanted to talk to you about a job."

"Great," I said. "That means his boss has got a new girl-friend, and I've got to paste on a new face."

She shook her head. "Viamount's taking over ILMGM and Arthurton's going to head Project Development, which means Mayer's boss is out, and Mayer's scrambling. He's got to dis-tance himself from his boss *and* convince Arthurton he should keep him instead of bringing in his own team. So this job is probably a bid to impress Arthurton, which could mean a re-make, or even a new project. In which case . . ."

I'd stopped listening. Mayer's boss was out, which meant the disk in my hand was worth exactly nothing, and the job he wanted to see me about was pasting Arthurton's girl-friend into something. Or maybe the girlfriends of the whole Viamount board of directors. Either way I wasn't going to get paid.

". . . in *which* case," Heada was saying, "his coming to you is a good sign."

"Golly," I said, clasping my hands together. " 'This could be my big break.' "

"Well, it could," she said defensively. "Even a remake would be better than these pimping jobs you've been doing."

"They're all pimping jobs." I started through the crush toward Mayer.

Heada squeezed through after me. "If it *is* an official project," she said, "tell him you want a credit."

Mayer had moved to the other side of the freescreen, probably trying to get away from Vincent, who was right behind him, still talking. Above them, the crowd on the screen was still revolving, but slower and slower, and the edges of the room were starting to soft-focus. Mayer turned and saw me, and waved, all in slow motion.

I stopped, and Heada crashed into me. "Do you have any slalom?" I said, and she started fumbling in her hand again. "Or ice? Anything to hold off a klieg flash?"

She held out the same assortment of capsules and cubes as before, only not as many. "I don't think so," she said, peering at them.

"Find me something, okay?" I said, and squeezed my eyes shut, hard, and then opened them again. The soft-focus receded.

"I'll see if I can find you some lude," she said. "Remember, if it's the real thing, you want a credit." She slipped off toward a pair of James Deans, and I went up to Mayer.

"Here you go," I said to Mayer, and tried to hand him the disk. I wasn't going to get paid, but it was at least worth a try.

"Tom!" Mayer said. He didn't take the disk.

Heada was right. His boss was out.

"Just the guy I've been looking for," he said. "What have you been up to?"

"Working for you," I said, and tried again to hand him the disk. "It's all done. Just what you ordered. River Phoenix, close-up, kiss. She's even got four lines."

"Great," he said, and pocketed the disk. He pulled out a palmtop and punched in numbers. "You want this in your on-line account, right?"

"Right," I said, wondering if this was some kind of bizarre pre-flashing symptom: actually getting what you wanted. I looked around for Heada. She wasn't talking to the James Deans anymore.

"I can always count on you for the tough jobs," Mayer said. "I've got a new project you might be interested in." He put a friendly arm around my shoulder and led me away from Vincent. "Nobody knows this," he said, "but there's a possibility of a merger between ILMGM and Viamount, and if it goes through, my boss and his girlfriends'll be a dead issue."

How does Heada do it? I thought wonderingly.

"It's still just in the talking stages, of course, but we're all very excited about the prospect of working with a great company like Viamount."

Translation: It's a done deal, and scrambling isn't even the word. I looked down at Mayer's hands, half expecting to see blood under his fingernails.

"Viamount's as committed as ILMGM is to the making of quality movies, but you know how the American public is about mergers. So our first job, *if* this thing goes through, is to send them the message: 'We care.' Do you know Austin Arthurton?"

Sorry, Heada, I thought, it's another pimping job.

"What's the job?" I said. "Didging in Arthurton's girlfriend? Boyfriend? German shepherd?"

"Jesus, no!" he said, and looked around to make sure nobody'd heard that. "Arthurton's totally straight, vegetarian, clean, a real Gary Cooper type. He's completely committed to convincing the public the studio's in responsible hands. Which is where you come in. We'll supply you with a memory upgrade and automatic print-and-send, and I'll have you paid on receipt through the feed." He waved the disk of his old boss's girlfriend at me. "No more having to track me down at parties." He smiled.

"What's the job?"

He didn't answer. He looked around the room, twitching. "I see a lot of new faces," he said, smiling at a Marilyn in yellow feathers. *There's No Business Like Show Business.* "Anything interesting?"

Yes, up in my room, and I want to flash on her, not you, Mayer, so get to the point.

"ILMGM's taken some flack lately. You know the rap: violence, AS's, negative influence. Nothing serious, but Arthurton wants to project a positive image—''

And he's a real Gary Cooper type. I was wrong about its being a pimping job, Heada. It's a slash-and-burn.

''What does he want out?'' I said.

He started to twitch again. ''It's not a censorship job, just a few adjustments here and there. The average revision won't be more than ten frames. Each one'll take you maybe fifteen minutes, and most of them are simple deletes. The comp can do those automatically.''

''And I take out what? Sex? Chooch?''

''AS's. Twenty-five a movie, and you get paid whether you have to change anything or not. It'll keep you in chooch for a year.''

''How many movies?''

''Not that many. I don't know exactly.''

He reached in his suit pocket and handed me an opdisk like the one I'd given him. ''The menu's on here.''

''Everything? Cigarettes? Alcohol?''

''All addictive substances,'' he said, ''visuals, audios, and references. But the Anti-Smoking League's already taken the nicotine out, and most of the movies on the list have only got a couple of scenes that need to be reworked. A lot of them are already clean. All you'll have to do is watch them, do a print-and-send, and collect your money.''

Right. And then feed in access codes for two hours. A wipe was easy, five minutes tops, and a superimpose ten, even working from a vid. It was the accesses that were murder. Even my

River Phoenix—watching marathon was nothing compared to the hours I'd spend reading in accesses, working my way past authorization guards and ID-locks so the fibe-op source wouldn't automatically spit out the changes I'd made.

"No, thanks," I said, and tried to hand him back the disk. "Not without full access."

Mayer looked patient. "You know why the authorization codes are necessary."

Sure. So nobody can change a pixel of all those copyrighted movies, or harm a hair on the head of all those bought-and-paid-for stars. Except the studios.

"Sorry, Mayer. Not interested," I said, and started to walk away.

"Okay, okay," he said, twitching. "Fifty per and full exec access. I can't do anything about the fibe-op-feed ID-locks and the Film Preservation Society registration. But you can have complete freedom on the changes. No preapproval. You can be creative."

"Yeah," I said. "Creative."

"Is it a deal?" he said.

Heada was sidling past the screen, looking up at Fred and Ginger. They were in close-up, gazing into each other's eyes.

At least the job would pay enough for my tuition and my own AS's, instead of having to have Heada mooch for me, instead of taking klieg by mistake and having to worry about flashing on Mayer and carrying an indelible image of him around in my head forever. And they're all pimping jobs, in or out. Or official.

"Why not?" I said, and Heada came up. She took my hand and slipped a lude into it.

"Great," Mayer said. "I'll give you a list. You can do them in any order. A minimum of twelve a week."

I nodded. "I'll get right on it," I said, and started for the stairs, popping the lude as I went.

Heada pursued me to the foot of the stairs. "Did you get the job?"

"Yeah."

"Was it a remake?"

I didn't have time to listen to what she'd say when she found out it was a slash-and-burn. "Yeah," I said, and sprinted back up the stairs.

There really wasn't any hurry. The lude would give me half an hour at least and Alis was already on the bed. If she was still there. If she hadn't gotten her fill of Fred and Ginge and left.

The door was half-open the way I'd left it, which was either a good or a bad sign. I looked in. I could see the near bank. The array was blank. Thanks, Mayer. She's gone, and all I've got to show for it is a Hays Office list. If I'm lucky I'll get to flash on Walter Brennan taking a swig of rotgut whiskey.

I started to push the door open, and stopped. She was there, after all. I could see her reflection in the silvered screens. She was sitting on the bed, leaning forward, watching something. I pushed the door farther open so I could see what. The door scraped a little against the carpet, but she didn't move. She was watching the center screen. It was the only one on. She must not have been able to figure out the other screens from my hurried instructions, or maybe one screen was all she was used to back in Bedford Falls.

She was watching with that focused look she had had down-stairs, but it wasn't the Continental. It wasn't even Ginger dancing side by side with Fred. It was Eleanor Powell. She and Fred were tap-dancing on a dark polished floor. There were lights in the background, meant to look like stars, and the floor reflected them in long, shimmering trails of light.

Fred and Eleanor were in white—him in a suit, no tails, no top hat this time, her in a white dress with a knee-length skirt that swirled out when she swung into the turns. Her light brown hair was the same length as Alis's and was pulled back with a white headband that glittered, catching the light from the re-flections.

Fred and Eleanor were dancing side by side, casually, their arms only a little out to the sides for balance, their hands not even close to touching, matching each other step for step.

Alis had the sound off, but I didn't need to hear the taps, or the music, to know what this was. *Broadway Melody of 1940,* the second half of the "Begin the Beguine" number. The first half was a tango, formal jacket and long white dress, the kind of stuff Fred did with all his partners, except that he didn't have to cover for Eleanor Powell or maneuver fancy steps around her. She could dance as well as he did.

And the second half was this—no fancy dress, no fuss, the two of them dancing side by side, full-length shot and one long, unbroken take. He tapped a combination, she echoed it, snap-ping the steps out in precision time, he did another, she answered, neither of them looking at the other, each of them intent on the music.

Not intent. Wrong word. There was no concentration in them at all, no effort, they might have made up the whole routine just now as they stepped onto the polished floor, improvising as they went.

I stood there in the door, watching Alis watch them as she sat there on the edge of the bed, looking like sex was the farthest thing from her mind. Heada was right—this had been a bad idea. I should go back down to the party and find some face who wasn't locked at the knees, whose big ambition was to work as a warmbody for Columbia Tri-Star. The lude I'd just taken would hold off any flash long enough for me to talk one of the Marilyns into coming on cue.

And Ruby Keeler'd never miss me—she was oblivious to everything but Fred Astaire and Eleanor Powell, doing a series of rapid-fire tap breaks. She probably wouldn't even notice if I brought the Marilyn back up to the bed to pop. Which is what I should do, while I still had time.

But I didn't. I leaned against the door, watching Fred and Eleanor and Alis, watching Alis's reflection in the blank screens of the right-hand array. Fred and Eleanor were reflected in the screens, too, their images superimposed on Alis's intent face on the silver screens.

And intent wasn't the right word for her either. She had lost that alert, focused look she'd had watching the Continental, counting the steps, trying to memorize the combinations. She had gone beyond that, watching Fred and

Connie Willis

Eleanor dance side by side, their hands not touching, and they weren't counting either, they were lost in the effortless steps, in the easy turns, lost in the dancing, and so was Alis. Her face was absolutely still watching them, like a freeze frame, and Fred Astaire and Eleanor Powell were somehow still, too, even as they danced.

They tapped, turning, and Eleanor danced Fred back across the floor, facing him now but still not looking at him, her steps reflections of his, and then they were side by side again, swinging into a tap cadenza, their feet and the swirling skirt and the fake stars reflected in the polished floor, in the screens, in Alis's still face.

Eleanor swung into a turn, not looking at Fred, not having to, the turn perfectly matched to his, and they were side by side again, tapping in counterpoint, their hands almost touching, Eleanor's face as still as Alis's, intent, oblivious. Fred tapped out a ripple, and Eleanor repeated it, and glanced sideways over her shoulder and smiled at him, a smile of awareness and complicity and utter joy.

I flashed.

The klieg usually gives you at least a few seconds warning, enough time to do something to hold it off or at least close your eyes, but not this time. No warning, no telltale soft-focus, nothing.

One minute I was leaning against the door, watching Alis watch Fred and Eleanor tippity-tapping away, and the next: freeze frame, Cut! Print and Send, like a flashbulb going off in your face, only the afterimage is as clear as the picture, and it doesn't fade, it doesn't go away.

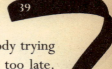

I put my hand up in front of my eyes, like somebody trying to shield themselves from a nuclear blast, but it was too late. The image was already burned into my neocortex.

I must've staggered back against the door, too, and maybe even cried out, because when I opened my eyes, she was looking at me, alarmed, concerned.

"Is something wrong?" she said, scrambling off the bed and taking my arm. "Are you okay?"

"I'm fine," I said. Fine. She was holding the remote. I took it away from her and clicked the comp off. The screen went silver, blank except for the reflection of the two of us standing there in the door. And superimposed on the reflection another reflection—Alis's face, rapt, absorbed, watching Fred and Eleanor in white, dancing on the starry floor.

"Come on," I said, and grabbed Alis's hand.

"Where are we going?"

Someplace. Anyplace. A theater where some other movie is showing. "Hollywood," I said, pulling her out into the hall. "To dance in the movies."

Camera whip-pans to medium-shot: LAIT station sign. Diamond screen, "Los Angeles Instransit" in hot pink caps, "Westwood Station" in bright green.

E TOOK THE SKIDS. MISTAKE. THE BACK SEC-tion was closed off but they were still practically empty—a few knots of tourates on their way home from Universal Studios clumped together in the middle of the room, a couple of druggates asleep against the back wall, three others over by the far side wall, laying out three-card monte hands on the yellow warning strip, one lone Marilyn.

The tourates were watching the station sign anxiously, like they were afraid they'd miss their stop. Fat chance. The time between Instransit stations may be inst, but it takes the skids a good ten minutes to generate the negative-matter region that produces the transit, and another five afterwards before they turn on the exit arrows, during which time nobody was going anywhere.

The tourates might as well relax and enjoy the show. What there was of it. Only one of the side walls was working, and half of it was running a continuous loop of ads for ILMGM, which apparently didn't know it'd been taken over yet. In the center of the wall, a digitized lion roared under the studio trademark in glowing gold: ''Anything's Possible!'' The screen blurred and went to swirling mist, while a voice-over said, ''ILMGM! More Stars Than There Are in Heaven,'' and then announced names while said stars appeared out of the fog. Vivien Leigh tripping toward us in a huge hoop skirt; Arnold Schwarzenegger roaring in on a motorcycle; Charlie Chaplin twirling his cane.

''Constantly working to bring you the brightest stars in the firmament,'' the voice-over said, which meant the stars currently in copyright litigation. Marlene Dietrich, Macaulay Culkin at age ten, Fred Astaire in top hat and tails, strolling effortlessly, casually toward us.

I'd dragged Alis out of the dorm to get away from mirrors and the Beguine and Fred, tippity-tapping away on my frontal lobe, to find something different to look at if I flashed again, but all I'd done was exchange my screen for a bigger one.

The other wall was even worse. It was apparently later than I'd thought. They'd shut the ads off for the night, and it was nothing but a long expanse of mirror. Like the polished floor Fred Astaire and Eleanor Powell had danced on, side by side, their hands nearly—

I focused on the reflections. The druggates looked dead. They'd probably taken capsules Heada told them were chooch. The Marilyn was practicing her pout in the mirror, flinching forward with a look of openmouthed surprise, and splaying her hand against her white pleated skirt to keep it from billowing up. The steam grating scene from *The Seven Year Itch*.

The tourates were still watching the station sign, which read La Brea Tar Pits. Alis was watching it, too, her face intent, and even in the fluorescents and the flickering light of ILMGM upcoming remakes, her hair had that curious backlit look. Her feet were apart, and she held her hands out, braced for sudden movement.

"No skids in Riverwood, huh?" I said.

She grinned. "Riverwood. That's Mickey Rooney's hometown in *Strike Up the Band*," she said. "We only had a little one in Galesburg. And it had seats."

"You can squeeze more people in during rush hour without seats. You don't have to stand like that, you know."

"I know," she said, moving her feet together. "I just keep expecting us to move."

"We already did," I said, glancing at the station sign. It had changed to Pasadena. "For about a nanosecond. Station to station and no in-between. It's all done with mirrors."

I stood on the yellow warning strip and put my hand out toward the side wall. "Only they're not mirrors. They're a curtain of negative matter you could put your hand right through. You need to get a studio exec on the make to explain it to you."

"Isn't it dangerous?" she said, looking down at the yellow warning strip.

"Not unless you try to walk through them, which ravers sometimes try to do. There used to be barriers, but the studios made them take them out. They got in the way of their promos."

She turned and looked at the far wall. "It's so big!"

"You should see it during the day. They shut off the back part at night. So the druggates don't piss on the floor. There's another room back there," I pointed at the rear wall, "that's twice as big as this."

"It's like a rehearsal hall," Alis said. "Like the dance studio in *Swingtime*. You could almost dance in here."

" 'I won't dance,' " I said. " 'Don't ask me.' "

"Wrong movie," she said, smiling. "That's from *Roberta*."

She turned back to the mirrored side wall, her skirt flaring out, and her reflection called up the image of Eleanor Powell next to Fred Astaire on the dark, polished floor, her hand—

I forced it back, staring determinedly at the other wall, where a trailer for the new *Star Trek* movie was flashing, till it receded, and then turned back to Alis.

She was looking at the station sign. Pasadena was flashing. A line of green arrows led to the front, and the tourates were following them through the left-hand exit door and off to Disneyland.

"Where are we going?" Alis said.

"Sight-seeing," I said. "The homes of the stars. Which

#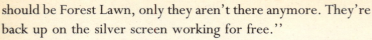

should be Forest Lawn, only they aren't there anymore. They're back up on the silver screen working for free.''

I waved my hand at the near wall, where a trailer for the remake of *Pretty Woman,* starring, natch, Marilyn Monroe, was showing.

Marilyn made an entrance in a red dress, and the Marilyn stopped practicing her pout and came over to watch. Marilyn flipped an escargot at a waiter, went shopping on Rodeo Drive for a white halter dress, faded out on a lingering kiss with Clark Gable.

''Appearing soon as Lena Lamont in *Singin' in the Rain,*'' I said. ''So tell me why you hate Gene Kelly.''

''I don't hate him exactly,'' she said, considering. ''*American in Paris* is awful, and that fantasy thing in *Singin' in the Rain,* but when he dances with Donald O'Connor and Frank Sinatra, he's actually a good dancer. It's just that he makes it look so *hard.*''

''And it isn't?''

''No, it *is.* That's the point.'' She frowned. ''When he does jumps or complicated steps, he flails his arms and puffs and pants. It's like he wants you to know how hard it is. Fred Astaire doesn't do that. His routines are lots harder than Gene Kelly's, the steps are *terrible,* but you don't see any of that on the screen. When he dances, it doesn't look like he's working at all. It looks easy, like he just that minute made it up——''

The image of Fred and Eleanor pushed forward again, the two of them in white, tapping casually, effortlessly, across the starry floor——

"And he made it look so easy you thought you'd come to Hollywood and do it, too," I said.

"I know it won't be easy," she said quietly. "I know there aren't a lot of liveactions——"

"*Any,*" I said. "There aren't *any* liveactions being made. Unless you're in Bogota. Or Beijing. It's all CGs. No actors need apply."

Dancers either, I thought, but didn't say it. I was still hoping to get a pop out of this, if I could hang onto her till the next flash. If there was a next flash. I was getting a killing headache, which wasn't supposed to be a side-effect.

"But if it's all computer graphics," Alis was saying earnestly, "then they can do whatever they want. Including musicals."

"And what makes you think they want to? There hasn't been a musical since 1996."

"They're copyrighting Fred Astaire," she said, gesturing at the screen. "They must want him for something."

Something is right, I thought. The sequel to *The Towering Inferno*. Or snuffporn movies.

"I said I knew it wouldn't be easy," she said defensively. "You know what they said about Fred Astaire when he first came to Hollywood? Everybody said he was washed up, that his sister was the one with all the talent, that he was a no-talent vaudeville hoofer who'd never make it in movies. On his screen test somebody wrote, 'Thirty, balding, can dance a little.' They didn't think he could do it either, and look what happened."

There were movies for him to dance in, I didn't say, but she

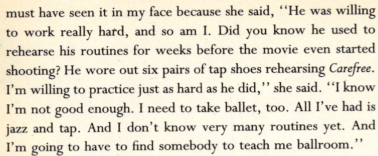

must have seen it in my face because she said, "He was willing to work really hard, and so am I. Did you know he used to rehearse his routines for weeks before the movie even started shooting? He wore out six pairs of tap shoes rehearsing *Carefree*. I'm willing to practice just as hard as he did," she said. "I know I'm not good enough. I need to take ballet, too. All I've had is jazz and tap. And I don't know very many routines yet. And I'm going to have to find somebody to teach me ballroom."

Where? I thought. There hasn't been a dancing teacher in Hollywood in twenty years. Or a choreographer. Or a musical. CGs might have killed the liveaction, but they hadn't killed the musical. It had died all by itself back in the sixties.

"I'll need a job to pay for the dancing lessons, too," she was saying. "The girl you were talking to at the party—the one who looks like Marilyn Monroe—she said maybe I could get a job as a face. What do they do?"

Go to parties, stand around trying to get noticed by somebody who'll trade a pop for a paste-up, do chooch, I thought, wishing I had some.

"They smile and talk and look sad while some hackate does a scan of them," I said.

"Like a screen test?" Alis said.

"Like a screen test. Then the hackate digitizes the scan of your face and puts it into a remake of *A Star Is Born* and you get to be the next Judy Garland. Only why do that when the studio's already got Judy Garland? And Barbra Streisand. And Janet Gaynor. And they're all copyrighted, they're already stars, so why would the studios take a chance on a new face? And why

take a chance on a new movie when they can do a sequel or a
copy or a remake of something they already own? And while
we're at it, why not *star* remakes in the remake? Hollywood,
the ultimate recycler!''

I waved my hand at the screen where ILMGM was touting
coming attractions. ''*The Phantom of the Opera*,'' the voice-over
said. ''Starring Anthony Hopkins and Meg Ryan.''

''Look at that,'' I said. ''Hollywood's latest effort—a remake of a remake of a silent!''

The trailer ended, and the loop started again. The digitized
lion did its digitized roar, and above it a digitized laser burned
in gold: ''Anything's Possible!''

''Anything's possible,'' I said, ''if you have the digitizers and
the Crays and the memory and the fibe-op feed to send it out
over. And the copyrights.''

The golden words faded into fog, and Scarlett simpered her
way out of it towards us, holding up her hoop skirt daintily.

''Anything's possible, but only for the studios. They own
everything, they control everything, they—''

I broke off, thinking, there's no way she'll give me a pop
after that little outburst. Why didn't you just tell her straight
out her little dream's impossible?

But she wasn't listening. She was looking at the screen,
where the copyright cases were being trotted out for inspection.
Waiting for Fred Astaire to appear.

''The first time I ever saw him, I knew what I wanted,'' she
said, her eyes on the wall. ''Only 'wanted' isn't the right word.
I mean, not like you want a new dress—''

"Or some chooch," I said.

"It's not even that kind of wanting. It's . . . there's a scene in *Top Hat* where Fred Astaire's dancing in his hotel room and Ginger Rogers has the room below him, and she comes up to complain about the noise, and he tells her that sometimes he just finds himself dancing, and *she* says—"

" 'I suppose it's a kind of affliction,' " I said.

I'd expected her to smile at that, the way she had at my other movie quotes, but she didn't.

"An affliction," she said seriously. "Only that isn't it either, exactly. It's . . . when he dances, it isn't just that he makes it look easy. It's like all the steps and rehearsing and the music are just practice, and what he does is the real thing. It's like he's gone beyond the rhythm and the time steps and the turns to this other place. . . . If I could get there, do that . . ."

She stopped. Fred Astaire was sauntering toward us out of the mist in his top hat and tails, tipping his top hat jauntily forward with the end of his cane. I looked at Alis.

She was looking at him with that lost, breathless look she had had in my room, watching Fred and Eleanor, side by side, dressed in white, turning and yet still, silent, beyond motion, beyond—

"Come on," I said, and yanked on her hand. "This is our stop," and followed the green arrows out.

SCENE: *Hollywood premiere night at Grauman's Chinese Theatre. Searchlights crisscrossing the night sky, palm trees, screaming fans, limousines, tuxedos, furs, flashbulbs popping.*

*W*E CAME OUT ON HOLLYWOOD BOULEVARD, on the corner of Chaos and Sensory Overload, the worst possible place to flash.

It was a DeMille scene, as usual. Faces and tourates and freelancers and ravers and thousands of extras, milling among the vid places and VR caves. And among the screens: drops and freescreens and diamonds and holos, all showing trailers edited à la *Psycho* by Vincent.

Trump's Chinese Theater had two huge dropscreens in front of it, running promos of the latest remake of *Ben-Hur*. On one of them, Sylvester Stallone in a bronze skirt and digitized sweat was leaning over his chariot, whipping the horses.

You couldn't see the other. There was a vid-neon sign in front of it that said Happy Endings, and a holoscreen showing

Scarlett O'Hara in the fog, saying, "But, Rhett, I love you."

"Frankly, my dear—I love you, too," Clark Gable said, and crushed her in his arms. "I've always loved you!"

"The cement has stars in it," I said to Alis, pointing down. It was too crowded to see the sidewalk, let alone the stars. I led her out into the street, which was just as crowded, but at least it was moving, and down toward the vid places.

Hawkers from the VR caves crushed flyers into our hands, two dollars off reality, and River Phoenix pushed up. "Drag? Flake? A pop?"

I bought some chooch and popped it right there, hoping it would stave off a flash till we got back to the dorm.

The crowd thinned out a little, and I led Alis back onto the sidewalk and past a VR cave advertising, "A hundred percent body hookup! A hundred percent realistic!"

A hundred percent realistic, all right. According to Heada, who knows everything, simsex takes more memory than most of the VR caves can afford, and half of them slap a data helmet on the customer, add some noise to make it look like a VR image, and bring in a freelancer.

I towed Alis around the VR cave and straight into a herd of tourates standing in front of a booth called A Star Is Born and gawking at a vid-pitch. "Make your dreams come true! Be a movie star! $89.95, including disk. Studio-licensed! Studio-quality digitizing!"

"I don't know, which one do you think I should do?" a fat female tourate was saying, flipping through the menu.

A bored-looking hackate in a white lab coat and James Dean pompadour glanced at the movie she was pointing at, handed her a plastic bundle, and motioned her into a curtained cubicle.

She stopped halfway in. "I'll be able to watch this on the fibe-op feed, won't I?"

"Sure," James Dean said, and yanked the curtain across.

"Do you have any musicals?" I asked, wondering if he'd lie to me like he had to the tourate. She wasn't going to be on the fibe-op feed. Nothing gets on except studio-authorized changes. Paste-ups and slash-and-burns. She'd get a tape of the scene and orders not to make any copies.

He looked blank. "Musicals?"

"You know. Singing? Dancing?" I said, but the tourate was back wearing a too-short white robe and a brown wig with braids looped over her ears.

"Stand up here," James Dean said, pointing at a plastic crate. He fastened a data harness around her large middle and went over to an old Digimatte compositor and switched it on.

"Look at the screen," he said, and the tourates all moved so they could see it. Storm troopers blasted away, and Luke Skywalker appeared, standing in a doorway over a dropoff, his arm around a blank blue space in the screen.

I left Alis watching and pushed through the crowd to the menu. *Stagecoach, The Godfather, Rebel without a Cause.*

"Okay, now," James Dean said, typing onto a keyboard. The female tourate appeared on the screen next to Luke. "Kiss him on the cheek and step off the box. You don't have to jump. The data harness'll do everything."

"Won't it show in the movie?"

"The machine cuts it out."

They didn't have any musicals. Not even Ruby Keeler. I worked my way back to Alis.

"Okay, roll 'em," James Dean said. The fat tourate smooched empty air, giggled, and jumped off the box. On the screen, she kissed Luke's cheek, and they swung out across a high-tech abyss.

"Come on," I said to Alis and steered her across the street to Screen Test City.

It had a multiscreen filled with stars' faces, and an old guy with the pinpoint eyes of a redliner. "Be a star! Get your face up on the silver screen! Who do you want to be, popsy?" he said, leering at Alis. "Marilyn Monroe?"

Ginger Rogers and Fred Astaire were side by side on the bottom row of the screen. "That one," I said, and the screen zoomed till they filled it.

"You're lucky you came tonight," the old guy said. "He's going into litigation. What do you want? Still or scene?"

"Scene," I said. "Just her. Not both of us."

"Stand in front of the scanner," he said, pointing, "and let me get a still of your smile."

"No, thank you," Alis said, looking at me.

"Come on," I said. "You said you wanted to dance in the movies. Here's your chance."

"You don't have to do anything," the old guy said. "All I need's an image to digitize from. The scanner does the rest. You don't even have to smile."

He took hold of her arm, and I expected her to wrench away from him, but she didn't move.

"I want to dance in the movies," she said, looking at me, "not get my face digitized onto Ginger Rogers's body. I want to dance."

"You'll be dancing," the old guy said. "Up there on the screen for everybody to see." He waved his free hand at the milling cast of thousands, none of whom were looking at his screen. "And on opdisk."

"You don't understand," she said to me, tears welling up in her eyes. "The CG revolution—"

"Is right there in front of you," I said, suddenly fed up. "Simsex, paste-ups, snuffshows, make-your-own remakes. Look around, Ruby. You want to dance in the movies? This is as close as you're going to get!"

"I thought you understood," she said bleakly, and whirled before either of us could stop her, and plunged into the crowd.

"Alis, wait!" I shouted, and started after her, but she was already far ahead. She disappeared into the entrance to the skids.

"Lose the girl?" a voice said, and I turned and glared. I was opposite the Happy Endings booth. "Get dumped? Change the ending. Make Rhett come back to Scarlett. Make Lassie come home."

I crossed the street. It was all simsex parlors on this side, promising a pop with Mel Gibson, Sharon Stone, the Marx Brothers. A hundred percent realistic. I wondered if I should do a sim. I stuck my head in the promo data helmet, but there wasn't any blurring. The chooch must be working.

"You shouldn't do that," a female voice said.

I pulled my head out of the helmet. A freelancer was standing there, blond, in a torn net leotard and a beauty mark. *Bus Stop*. "Why go for a virtual imitation when you can have the real thing?" she breathed.

"Which is what?" I said.

The smile didn't fade, but she looked instantly on guard. Mary Astor in *The Maltese Falcon*. "What?"

"This real thing. What is it? Sex? Love? Chooch?"

She half put up her hands, like she was being arrested. "Are you a narc? 'Cause I don't know what you're talking about. I was just making a comment, okay? I just don't think people should settle for VRs, is all, when they could talk to somebody real."

"Like Marilyn Monroe?" I said, and wandered on down the sidewalk past three more freelancers. Marilyn in a white halter dress, Madonna in brass cones, Marilyn in pink satin. The real thing.

I scored some more chooch and a line of tinseltown from a James Dean too splatted to remember he was supposed to be selling the stuff, and ate it, walking on past the snuffshows, but somewhere I must have gotten turned around because I was back at Happy Endings, watching the holoscreen. Scarlett ran into the fog after Rhett, Butch and Sundance leaped forward into a hail of gunfire, Humphrey Bogart and Ingrid Bergman stood in front of an airplane looking at each other.

"Back again, huh?" the hawker said. "Best thing for a broken heart. Kill the bastards. Get the girl. What'll it be? *Lost Horizon? Terminator 9?*"

Ingrid was telling Bogie she wanted to stay, and Bogie was telling her it was impossible.

"What happy endings do people come up with for this?" I asked him.

"*Casablanca?*" He shrugged. "The Nazis show up and kill the husband, Ingrid and Bogart get married."

"And honeymoon in Auschwitz," I said.

"I didn't say the endings were any good."

On the screen Bogie and Ingrid were looking at each other. Tears welled up in her eyes, and the edges of the screen went to soft-focus.

"How about *Shadowlands?*" the guy said, but I was already shoving through the crowd, trying to reach the skids before I flashed.

I almost made it. I was past the chariot race when a Marilyn crashed into me and I went down, and I thought, natch, I'm going to flash on cement, but I didn't.

The sidewalk blurred and then went blinding, and there were stars in it, and Fred and Eleanor, all in white, danced easily, elegantly through the milling crowd, and superimposed across them was Alis, watching them, her face lost and sorrowful. Like Ingrid's.

Fade to Black

MONTAGE: *No sound, HERO, seated at comp, punches keys and deletes AS's as scene on screen changes. Western saloon, elegant nightclub, fraternity house, waterfront bar.*

W HATEVER EFFECT MY JUDGE HARDY LECTURE had had on Alis, it didn't make her give up on her dream and head back to Meadowville. She was at the party again the next week.

I wasn't. I'd gotten Mayer's list and a notice that my scholarship had been canceled due to "nonperformance," and I was working on Mayer's list just to stay in the dorm. And in chooch.

I didn't miss anything, though. Heada came up to my room halfway through the party to fill me in. "The takeover's definitely on," she said. "Mayer's boss's been moved to Development, which means he's on the way out. Warner's filing a countersuit on Fred Astaire. It goes to court tomorrow."

Alis should have had her face pasted onto Ginger's while she had the chance. She'd never get a chance to dance with him now.

"Vincent's at the party," she said. "He's got a new decay morph."

"What a pity I've got to miss that," I said.

"What are you doing up here anyway?" she said, fishing. "You've never missed a party before. Everybody's down there. Mayer, Alis—" she paused, watching my face.

"Mayer, huh?" I said. "I've got to talk to him about a raise. Do you know who drinks in the movies? Everybody." I took a swig of scotch to illustrate. "Even Gary Cooper."

"Should you be doing that stuff?" Heada said.

"Are you kidding? It's cheap, it's legal, *and* I know what it is." And it was pretty good at keeping me from flashing.

"Is it safe?" Heada, who thought nothing of snorting white stuff she found on the floor, was reading the bottle warily.

"Of course it's safe. *And* endorsed by W. C. Fields, John Barrymore, Bette Davis, and E.T. And the major studios. It's in every movie on Mayer's list. *Camille, The Maltese Falcon, Gunga Din.* Even *Singin' in the Rain.* Champagne at the party after the premiere." The one where Donald O'Connor said, "You have to show a movie at a party. It's a Hollywood law."

I finished off the bottle. "Also *Oklahoma!* Poor Judd is dead. Dead drunk."

"Mayer was hitting on Alis at the party," she said, still looking at me.

Yeah, well, that was inevitable.

"Alis was telling him how she wanted to dance in the movies."

That was inevitable, too.

"I hope they'll be very happy," I said. "Or is he saving her to give to Gary Cooper?"

"She can't find a dancing teacher."

"Well, I'd love to stay and chat," I said, "but I've got to get back to the Hays Office." I called up *Casablanca* again and started deleting liquor bottles.

"I think you should help her," Heada said.

"Sorry," I said. " 'I stick my neck out for nobody.' "

"That's a quote from a movie, isn't it?"

"Bingo," I said. I deleted the crystal decanter Humphrey Bogart was pouring himself a drink out of.

"I think you should find her a dancing teacher. You know a lot of people in the business."

"There *aren't* any people in the business. It's all CGs, it's all ones and zeros and didge-actors and edit programs. The studios aren't even hiring warmbodies anymore. The only *people* in the business are dead, along with the liveaction. Along with the musical. Kaput. Over. 'The end of Rico.' "

"That's a quote from the movies, too, isn't it?"

"Yes," I said, "which are also dead in case you couldn't tell from Vincent's decay morph."

"You could get her a job as a face."

"Like the one you've got?"

"Well, then, a job as a hackate, as a foley, or a location assistant or something. She knows a lot about movies."

"She doesn't want to hack," I said, "and even if she did, the only movies she knows about are musicals. A location assistant's got to know everything, stock shots, props, frame numbers. Be a perfect job for you, Heada. Now I really have to get back to playing Lee Remick."

Heada looked like she wanted to ask if that was a movie, too.

"*Hallelujah Trail,*" I said. "Temperance leader, battling demon rum." I tipped the bottle up, trying to get the last drops out. "You have any chooch?"

She looked uncomfortable. "No."

"Well, what have you got? Besides klieg. I don't need any more doses of reality."

"I don't have anything," she said, and blushed. "I'm trying to taper off a little."

"You?!" I said. "What happened? Vincent's decay morph get to you?"

"No," she said defensively. "The other night, when I was on the klieg, I was listening to Alis talk about wanting to be a dancer, and I suddenly realized there was nothing I wanted, except chooch and getting popped."

"So you decided to go straight, and now you and Alis are going to tap-dance your way to stardom. I can see it now, your names up in lights——Ruby Keeler and Una Merkel in *Gold Diggers of 2018*!"

"*No,*" she said, "but I decided I'd like to be like her, that I'd like to want something."

"Even if that something is impossible?"

I couldn't make out her expression. "Yeah."

"Well, giving up chooch isn't the way to do it. If you want to figure out what it is you want, the way to do it is to watch a lot of movies."

She looked defensive again.

"How do you think Alis came up with this dancing thing? From the movies. She doesn't just want to dance in the movies, she wants to be Ruby Keeler in *42nd Street*—the plucky little chorus girl with a heart of gold. The odds are stacked against her, and all she's got is determination and a pair of tap shoes, but don't worry. All she has to do is keep hoofing and hoping, and she'll not only make it big, she'll save the show *and* get Dick Powell. It's all right there in the script. You didn't think Alis came up with it on her own, did you?"

"Came up with what?"

"Her *part*," I said. "That's what the movies do. They don't entertain us, they don't send the message: 'We care.' They give us lines to say, they assign us parts: John Wayne, Theda Bara, Shirley Temple, take your pick."

I waved at the screen, where the Nazi commandant was ordering a bottle of Veuve Cliquot '26 he wasn't going to get to drink. "How about Claude Rains sucking up to the Nazis? No, sorry, Mayer's already playing that part. But don't worry, there are enough parts to go around, and everybody's got a featured role, whether they know it or not, even the faces. They think they're playing Marilyn, but they're not. They're doing Greta Garbo as Sadie Thompson. Why do you think the execs keep doing all these remakes? Why do they keep hiring Humphrey

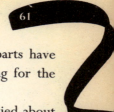

Bogart and Bette Davis? It's because all the good parts have already been cast, and all we're doing is auditioning for the remake.''

She looked at me so intently I wondered if she'd lied about giving up AS's and was doing klieg. ''Alis was right,'' she said. ''You do love the movies.''

''What?''

''I never noticed, the whole time I've known you, but she's right. You know all the lines and all the actors, and you're always quoting from them. Alis says you act like you don't care, but underneath you really love them, or you wouldn't know them all by heart.''

I said, in my best Claude Rains, '' 'Ricky, I think that underneath that cynical shell you are quite the sentimentalist.' Ruby Keeler does Ingrid Bergman in *Spellbound*. Did Dr. Bergman have any other psychiatric observations?''

''She said that's why you do so many AS's, because you love movies and you can't stand seeing them being butchered.''

''Wrong,'' I said. ''You don't know everything, Heada. It's because I pushed Gregory Peck onto a spiked fence when we were kids.''

''See?'' she said wonderingly. ''Even when you're denying it, you do it.''

''Well, this has been fun, but I have to get back to work butchering,'' I said, ''and you have to get back to deciding whether you want to play Sadie Thompson or Una Merkel.'' I turned back to the screen. Peter Lorre was clutching Humphrey Bogart's lapels, begging him to save him.

"You said everybody's playing a part, whether they know it or not," Heada said. "What part am I playing?"

"Right now? Thelma Ritter in *Rear Window*. The meddling friend who doesn't know when to keep her nose out of other people's business," I said. "Shut the door when you leave."

She did, and then opened it again and stood there watching me. "Tom?"

"Yeah?" I said.

"If I'm Thelma Ritter and Alis is Ruby Keeler, what part are you playing?"

"King Kong."

Heada left, and I sat there for a while, watching Humphrey Bogart stand by and let Peter Lorre get arrested, and then got up to see if there were any AS's on the premises. There was klieg in the medicine cabinet, just what I needed, and a bottle of champagne from one time when Mayer brought a face up to watch me paste her into *East of Eden*. I took a swig. It was flat, but better than nothing. I poured some in a glass and ff'd to the "Play it again, Sam" scene.

Bogart slugged down a drink, the screen went to soft-focus, and he was pouring Ingrid Bergman champagne in front of a matte that was supposed to be Paris.

The door opened.

"Forget to give me some gossip, Heada?" I said, taking another swallow.

It was Alis. She was wearing a pinafore and puffed sleeves. Her hair was darker, and had a big bow in it, but it had that same backlit look to it, framing her face with radiance.

Fred Astaire tapped a ripple on the polished floor, and Eleanor Powell repeated it and turned to smile at him—

I downed the rest of the champagne in one gulp, and poured some more. "Well, if it isn't Ruby Keeler," I said. "What do you want?"

She stayed in the doorway. "The musicals you showed me the other night, Heada said you might be willing to loan me the opdisks."

I took a drink of champagne. "They aren't on disk. It's a direct fibe-op feed," I said, and sat down at the comp.

"Is that what you do?" she said from behind me. She was standing looking over my shoulder at the screen. "You ruin movies?"

"That's what I do," I said. "I protect the movie-going public from the evils of demon rum and chooch. Mostly demon rum. There aren't all that many movies with drugs in them. *Valley of the Dolls, Postcards from the Edge,* a couple of Cheech and Chongs, *The Thief of Bagdad.* I also remove nicotine if the Anti-Smoking League didn't get there first." I deleted the champagne glass Ingrid Bergman was raising to her lips. "What do you think? Cocoa or tea?"

She didn't say anything.

"It's a big job. Maybe you could do the musicals. Want me to access Mayer and see if he'll hire you?"

She looked stubborn. "Heada said you could make opdisks for me off the feed," she said stiffly. "I just need them to practice with. Till I can find a dancing teacher."

I turned around in the chair to look at her. "And then what?"

Connie Willis

"If you don't want to lend them to me, I could watch them here and copy down the steps. When you're not using the comp."

"And then what?" I said. "You copy down the steps and practice the routines and then what? Gene Kelly pulls you out of the chorus—no, wait, I forgot, you don't like Gene Kelly—Gene Nelson pulls you out of the chorus and gives you the lead? Mickey Rooney decides to put on a show? What?"

"I don't know. When I find a dancing teacher—"

"There *aren't* any dancing teachers. They all went home to Meadowville fifteen years ago, when the studios switched to computer animation. There aren't any soundstages or rehearsal halls or studio orchestras. There aren't any *studios,* for God's sake! All there is is a bunch of geekates hacking away on Crays and a bunch of corporation execs telling 'em what to do. Let me show you something." I twisted back around in the chair. "Menu," I said. "*Top Hat.* Frame 97-265."

Fred and Ginge came up on the screen, spinning around in the Piccolino. "You want to bring musicals back. We'll do it right here. Forward at five." The screen slowed to a sequence of frames. Kick and. Turn and. Lift.

"How long did you say Fred had to practice his routines?"

"Six weeks," she said tonelessly.

"Too long. Think of all that rehearsal-hall rent. And all those tap shoes. Frame 97-288 to 97-631, repeat four times, then 99-006 to 99-115, and continuous loop. At twenty-four." The screen slid into realtime, and Fred lifted Ginge, lifted her again, and again, effortlessly, lightly. Lift, and lift, and kick and turn.

"Does that kick look high enough to you?" I said, pointing at the screen. "Frame 99-108 and freeze." I fiddled with the image, raising Fred's leg till it touched his nose. "Too high?" I eased it back down a little, smoothed out the shadows. "Forward at twenty-four."

Fred kicked, his leg sailing into the air. And lift. And lift. And lift. And lift.

"All right," Alis said. "I get the point."

"Bored already? You're right. This should be a production number." I hit multiply. "Eleven, side by side," I said, and a dozen Fred Astaires kicked in perfect synch, lift, and lift, and lift, and lift. "Multiply rows," I said, and the screen filled with Fred, lifting, kicking, tipping his top hat.

I turned around to look at Alis. "Why would they want you when they can have Fred Astaire? A hundred Fred Astaires? A thousand? And none of them have trouble learning a step, none of them get blisters on their feet or throw temper tantrums or have to be paid or get old or—"

"Get drunk," she said.

"You want Fred drunk?" I said. "I can do that, too. Frame 97-412 and freeze." Fred Astaire stopped in midturn, smiling. "Frame 97—" I said, and the screen went silver and then to legalese. "The character of Fred Astaire is currently unavailable for fibe-op transmission. Copyright ownership suit *ILMGM* v. *RKO-Warner* . . ."

"Oops. Fred's in litigation. Too bad. You should have taken that paste-up while you had the chance."

She wasn't looking at the screen. She was looking at me, her gaze alert, focused, the way it had been on the Piccolino. "If you're so sure what I want is impossible, why are you trying so hard to talk me out of it?"

Because I don't want to see you down on Hollywood Boulevard in a torn-net leotard. I don't want to have to stick your face in a River Phoenix movie so Mayer's boss can pop you.

"You're right," I said. "Why the hell am I?" I turned to the comp and said, "Print accesses, all files." I ripped the hardcopy out of the printer. "Here. Take my fibe-op accesses and make all the disks you want. Practice till your little feet bleed." I thrust it at her.

She didn't take it.

"Go on," I said, and pressed it into her unresponsive hand. "Who am I to stand in your way? In the immortal words of Leo the Lion, anything's possible. Who cares if the studios have got all the copyrights and the fibe-op sources and the digitizers and the accesses? We'll sew our own costumes. We'll build our own sets. And then, right before we open, Bebe Daniels'll break her leg and you'll have to go on for her!"

She crumpled up the hardcopy, looking like she'd like to throw it at me. "How would you know what's possible and impossible? You don't even *try*. Fred Astaire—"

"Is tied up in court, but don't let that stop you. There's still Ann Miller. And *Seven Brides for Seven Brothers*. And Gene Kelly. Oh, wait, I forgot, you're too good for Gene Kelly. Tommy Tune. And don't forget Ruby Keeler."

She threw it.

I picked the hardcopy up and uncrumpled it. " 'Temper,

"Great," I said. "Alis can go back to the thirties and take dancing lessons from Busby Berkeley himself."

Only she didn't like Busby Berkeley, and after taking all the AS's out of *Footlight Parade* and *Gold Diggers of 1933,* neither did I.

She was right about there not being any dancing in his movies. There was a glimpse of tapping feet in *42nd Street,* a rehearsal going on in the background of a plot exposition scene, a few bars in "Pettin' in the Park" for Ruby, who danced about as well as Judy Garland. Otherwise it was all neon violins and revolving wedding cakes and fountains and posed platinum-haired chorus girls, every one of whom had probably been a studio exec's popsy. Overhead kaleidoscope shots and pans and low-angle shots from underneath chorus girls' spread-apart legs that would have given the Hays Office fits. But no dancing.

Lots of drinking, though—speakeasies and backstage parties and silver flasks stuck in chorus girls' garters. Even a production number in a bar, with Ruby Keeler as Shanghai Lil, a popsy who'd done a lot of hooch and a lot of sailors. A hymn to alcohol's finer qualities.

Of which there were many. It was cheap, it didn't do as much damage as redline, and if it didn't give you the blessed forgetfulness of chooch, it stopped the flashing and put a nice soft-focus on things in general. Which made it easier to work on Mayer's list.

It also came in assorted flavors—martinis for *Topper,* elderberry wine for *Arsenic and Old Lace,* a nice Chianti for *Silence of the Lambs.* In between I drank champagne, which had apparently

Connie Willis

been in every movie ever made, and cursed Mayer, and deleted beakers and laboratory flasks from the cantina scene in *Star Wars*.

I went to the next party, and the one after that, but Alis wasn't there. Vincent was, demonstrating another program, and the studio exec, still pitching time travel to the Marilyns, and Heada.

"That stuff wasn't klieg after all," she told me. "It was some designer chooch from Brazil."

"Which explains why I keep hearing the Beguine," I said.

"Huh?"

"Nothing," I said, looking around the room. Vincent's program must be a weeper simulator. Jackie Cooper was up on the screen, in a battered top hat and a polka-dot tie, blubbering over his dead dog.

"She's not here," Heada said.

"I was looking for Mayer," I said. "He's going to have to pay me double for *The Philadelphia Story*. The thing's full of alcohol. Sherry before lunch, martinis out by the pool, champagne, cocktails, hangovers, ice packs. Cary Grant, Katharine Hepburn, Jimmy Stewart. The whole cast's stinking."

I took a swig from the crème de menthe I had left over from *Days of Wine and Roses*. "The visuals will take at least three weeks, and that doesn't include the lines. 'I have the hiccups. I wonder if I might borrow a drink.' "

"She was here earlier," Heada said. "One of the execs was hitting on her."

"No, no, *I* say, 'I wonder if I might borrow a drink,' and

you say, 'Certainly. Coals to Newcastle.' " I took another drink.

"Should you be doing so much alcohol?" Heada, the chooch queen, said.

"I have to," I said. "It's the bad effect of watching all these movies. Thank goodness ILMGM's remaking them so no one else will be corrupted." I drank some more crème de menthe.

Heada looked at me sharply, like she'd been doing klieg again. "ILMGM's doing a remake of *Time After Time*. The exec told Alis he thought he could get her a part in it."

"Great," I said, and went over to look at Vincent's program.

Audrey Hepburn was up on the screen now, standing in the rain and sobbing over her cat.

"This is our new tears program," Vincent said. "It's still in the experimental stage."

He said something to his remote, and the screen split. A computerized didge-actor sobbed alongside Audrey, clutching what looked like a yellow rug. Tears weren't the only thing in the experimental stage.

"Tears are the most difficult form of water simulation to do," Vincent said. The Tin Woodman was up there now, rusting his joints. "It's because tears aren't really water. They've got mucoproteins and lysozymes and a high salt content. It affects the index of refraction and makes them hard to reproduce," he said, sounding defensive.

He should. The didge-woodman's tears looked like Vaseline, oozing out of digitized eyes. "You ever program VRs?" I said. "Of, say, a movie scene like the one you used for the edit program a couple of weeks ago? The Fred Astaire and Ginger Rogers scene?''

''A virtual? Sure. I can do helmet and full-body data. Is this something you're working on for Mayer?''

''Yeah,'' I said. ''Could you have the person take, say, Ginger Rogers's place, so she's dancing with Fred Astaire?''

''Sure. Foot and knee hookups, nerve stimulators. It'll feel like she's really dancing.''

''Not feel like,'' I said. ''Can you make it so she actually dances?''

He thought about it awhile, frowning at the screen. The Tin Woodman had disappeared. Ingrid Bergman and Humphrey Bogart were at the airport saying good-bye.

''Maybe,'' Vincent said. ''I guess. We could put on some sole-sensors and rig a feedback enhance to exaggerate her body movements so she could shuffle her feet back and forth.''

I looked at the screen. There were tears welling up in Ingrid's eyes, glimmering like the real thing. They probably weren't. It was probably the eighth take, or the eighteenth, and a makeup girl had come out with glycerine drops or onion juice to get the right effect. It wasn't the tears that did it anyway. It was the face, that sweet, sad face that knew it could never have what it wanted.

''We could do sweat enhancers,'' Vincent said. ''Armpits, neck.''

''Never mind,'' I said, still watching Ingrid. The screen split and a didge-actress stood in front of a didge-airplane, oozing baby oil.

''How about a directional sound hookup for the taps and

endorphins?'' Vincent said. ''She'll swear she was really dancing with Gene Kelly.''

I drank the rest of the crème de menthe and handed him the empty bottle and then went back up to my room and hacked away at *The Philadelphia Story* for two more days, trying to think of a good reason for Jimmy Stewart to carry Katharine Hepburn and sing ''Somewhere Over the Rainbow'' without being sloshed, and pretending I needed one.

Mayer would hardly care, and neither would his tight-assed boss. And nobody else watched liveactions. If the plot didn't make sense, the hackates who did the remake could worry about it. They'd probably remake the remake anyway. Which was also on the list.

I called it up. *High Society*. Bing Crosby and Grace Kelly. Frank Sinatra playing Jimmy Stewart. I ff'd through the last half of it, searching for inspiration, but it was even more awash with AS's. *And* it was a musical. I went back to *Story* and tried again.

It was no use. Jimmy Stewart had to be drunk in the swimming pool scene to tell Katharine Hepburn he loved her. Katharine had to be drunk for her fiancé to dump her and for her to realize she still loved Cary Grant.

I gave up on the scene and went back to the one before it. It was just as bad. There was too much exposition to cut it, and most of it was in Jimmy Stewart's badly slurred voice. I rewound to the beginning of the scene and turned the sound up, getting a match so I could overdub his dialogue.

''You're still in love with her, aren't you?'' Jimmy Stewart said, leaning belligerently toward Cary Grant.

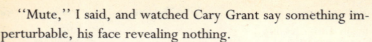

"Mute," I said, and watched Cary Grant say something imperturbable, his face revealing nothing.

"Insufficient," the comp said. "Additional match data needed."

"Yeah." I turned the sound up again.

"Liz says you are," Jimmy Stewart said.

I rew'd to the beginning of the scene and froze it for the frame number, and then went through the scene again.

"You're still in love with her, aren't you?" Jimmy Stewart said. "Liz says you are."

I blanked the screen, and accessed Heada. "I need to find out where Alis is," I said.

"Why?" she said suspiciously.

"I think I've found her a dancing teacher," I said. "I need her class schedule."

"Sorry," she said. "I don't know it."

"Come on, you know everything," I said. "What happened to 'I think you should help her'?"

"What happened to, 'I stick my neck out for nobody'?"

"I told you, I found her somebody to teach her to dance. An old woman out in Palo Alto. Ex–chorus girl. She was in *Finian's Rainbow* and *Funny Girl* back in the seventies."

She was still suspicious, but she gave it to me. Alis was taking Moviemaking 101, basic comp graphics stuff, and a film hist class, The Musical 1939–1980. It was clear out in Burbank.

I took the skids and a bottle of *Public Enemy* gin and went out to find her. The class was in an old studio building UCLA had bought when the skids were first built, on the second floor.

I opened the door a crack and looked in. The prof, who looked like Michael Caine in *Educating Rita,* a movie with way too many AS's in it, was standing in front of a blank, old-fashioned comp monitor with a remote, holding forth to a scattering of students, mostly hackates taking it for their movie content elective, some Marilyns, Alis.

"Contrary to popular belief, the computer graphics revolution didn't kill the musical," the prof said. "The musical kicked off," he paused to let the class titter, "in 1965."

He turned to the monitor, which was no bigger than my array screens, and clicked the remote. Behind him, cowboys appeared, leaping around a train station. *Oklahoma.*

"The musicals, with their contrived story lines, unrealistic song-and-dance sequences, and simplistic happy endings, no longer reflected the audience's world."

I glanced at Alis, wondering how she was taking this. She wasn't. She was watching the cowboys, with that intent, focused look, and her lips were moving, counting the beats, memorizing the steps.

" . . . which explains why the musical, unlike *film noir* and the horror movie, has not been revived in spite of the availability of such stars as Judy Garland and Gene Kelly. The musical is irrelevant. It has nothing to say to modern audiences. For example, *Broadway Melody of 1940* . . . "

I retreated up the uneven steps and sat there, working on the gin and waiting for him to finish. He did, finally, and the class trickled out. A trio of faces, talking about a rumor that Disney was going to use warmbodies in *Grand Hotel,* a couple of hackates, the prof, snorting flake on his way down the steps, another hackate.

I finished off the gin. Nobody else came out, and I wondered if I'd somehow missed Alis. I went to see. The steps had gotten steeper and more uneven while I sat there. I slipped once and grabbed onto the banister, and then stood there a minute, listening. There was a clatter and then a thunk from inside the room, and the faint sound of music. The janitor?

I opened the door and leaned against it.

Alis, in a sky-blue dress with a bustle, and a flowered hat, was dancing in the middle of the room, a blue parasol perched on her shoulder. A song was coming from the comp monitor, and Alis was high-stepping in time with a line of bustled, parasoled girls on the monitor behind her.

I didn't recognize the movie. *Carousel,* maybe? *The Harvey Girls?* The girls were replaced by high-stepping boys in derbies and straw hats, and Alis stopped, breathing hard, and pulled the remote out of her high-buttoned shoe. She rewound, stuck the remote back in her shoe, and propped the parasol against her shoulder. The girls appeared again, and Alis pointed her toe and did a turn.

She had piled the desks in stacks on either side of the room, but there still wasn't enough room. When she swung into the second turn, her outstretched hand crashed into them, nearly knocking them over. She reached for the remote again, rew'd, and saw me. She clicked the screen off and took a step backward. "What do you want?"

I waggled my finger at her. "Give you a little advice. 'Don't want what you can't have.' Michael J. Fox, *For Love or Money*. Bar scene, party, nightclub, three bottles of champagne. Only not anymore. Yours truly has done his job. Right down the sink.''

I swung my arm to demonstrate, like James Mason in *A Star Is Born,* and the chairs went over.

''You're splatted,'' she said.

'' 'Nope.' '' I grinned. ''Gary Cooper in *The Plainsman*.'' I walked toward her. ''Not splatted. Boiled, pickled, soused, sozzled. In a word, drunk as a skunk. It's a Hollywood tradition. Do you know how many movies have drinking in them? All. Except the ones I've taken it out of. *Dark Victory, Citizen Kane, Little Miss Marker.* Westerns, gangster movies, weepers. It's in all of them. Every one. Even *Broadway Melody of 1940.* Do you know why Fred got to dance the Beguine with Eleanor? Because George Murphy was too tanked up to go on. Forget dancing,'' I said, making another sweeping gesture that nearly hit her. ''What you need to do is have a drink.''

I tried to hand her the bottle.

She took another protective step toward the monitor. ''You're drunk.''

''Bingo,'' I said. '' 'Very drunk indeed,' as Audrey Hepburn would say. *Breakfast at Tiffany's.* A movie with a happy ending.''

''Why'd you come here?'' she said. ''What is it you want?''

I took a swig out of the bottle, remembered it was empty, and looked at it sadly. ''Came to tell you the movies aren't real life. Just because you want something doesn't mean you can have it. Came to tell you to go home before they remake you. Audrey should've gone home to Tulip, Texas. Came to tell you to go home to Carval.'' I waited, swaying, for her to get the reference.

''*Andy Hardy Has Too Much to Drink,*'' she said. ''He's the one who needs to go home.''

The screen faded to black for a few frames, and then I was sitting halfway down the steps, with Alis leaning over me. ''Are you all right?'' she said, and tears were glimmering in her eyes like stars.

''I'm fine,'' I said. '' 'Alcohol is the great level-el-ler,' as Jimmy Stewart would say. Need to pour some on these steps.''

''I don't think you should take the skids in your condition,'' she said.

''We're all on the skids,'' I said. ''Only place left.''

''Tom,'' she said, and there was another fade to black, and Fred and Ginger were on both walls, sipping martinis by the pool.

''That'll have to go,'' I said. ''Have to send the message 'We care.' Gotta sober Jimmy Stewart up. So what if it's the only way he can get up the courage to tell her what he really thinks? See, he knows she's too good for him. He knows he can't have her. He has to get drunk. Only way he can ever tell her he's in love with her.''

I put out my hand to her hair. ''How do you do that?'' I said. ''That backlighting thing?''

''Tom,'' she said.

I let my hand drop. "Doesn't matter. They'll ruin it in the remake. Not real anyway."

I waved my hand grandly at the screen like Gloria Swanson in *Sunset Boulevard*. "All a 'lusion. Makeup and wigs and fake sets. Even Tara. Just a false front. FX and foleys."

"I think you'd better sit down," Alis said, taking hold of my arm.

I shook it off. "Even Fred. Not the real thing at all. All those taps were dubbed in afterwards, and they aren't really stars. In the floor. It's all done with mirrors."

I lurched toward the wall. "Only it's not even a mirror. You can put your hand right through it."

After which things went to montage. I remember trying to get out at Forest Lawn to see where Holly Golightly was buried and Alis yanking on my arm and crying big jellied tears like the ones in Vincent's program. And something about the station sign beeping Beguine, and then we were back in my room, which looked funny, the arrays were on the wrong side of the room, and they all showed Fred carrying Eleanor over to the pool, and I said, "You know why the musical kicked off? Not enough drinking. Except Judy Garland," and Alis said, "Is he splatted?" and then answered herself, "No, he's drunk." And I said, " 'I don't want you to think I have a drinking problem. I can quit anytime. I just don't want to,' " and waited, grinning foolishly, for the two of them to get the reference, but they didn't. "*Some Like It Hot*, Marilyn Monroe," I said, and began to cry thick, oily tears. "Poor Marilyn."

And then I had Alis on the bed and was popping her and

watching her face so I'd see it when I flashed, but the flash
didn't come, and the room went to soft-focus around the edges,
and I pounded harder, faster, nailing her against the bed so she
couldn't get away, but she was already gone and I tried to go
after her and ran into the arrays, Fred and Eleanor saying good-
bye at the airport, and put my hand up and it went right through
and I lost my balance. But when I fell, it wasn't into Alis's arms
or into the arrays. It was into the negative-matter regions of
the skids.

LEWIS STONE: [*Sternly*] I hope you've learned your lesson, Andrew. Drinking doesn't solve your problems. It only makes them worse.

MICKEY ROONEY: [*Hangdog*] I know that now, Dad. And I've learned something else, too. I've learned I should mind my own business and not meddle in other people's affairs.

LEWIS STONE: [*Doubtfully*] I hope so, Andrew. I certainly hope so.

I N *THE PHILADELPHIA STORY,* KATHARINE HEPburn's getting drunk solved everything: her stuffed-shirt fiancé broke off the engagement, Jimmy Stewart quit tabloid journalism and started the serious novel his faithful girlfriend had always known he had in him, Mom and Dad reconciled, and Katharine Hepburn finally admitted she'd been in love with Cary Grant all along. Happy endings all around.

But the movies, as I had tried so soddenly to tell Alis, are not Real Life. And all I had done by getting drunk was to wake up in Heada's dorm room with a two-day hangover and a six-week suspension from the skids.

Not that I was going anywhere. Andy Hardy learns his lesson, forgets about girls, and settles down to the serious task of Minding His Own Business, a job made easier by the fact that Heada wouldn't tell me where Alis was because she wasn't speaking to me.

And by Heada's (or Alis's) pouring all my liquor down the drain like Katharine Hepburn in *The African Queen* and Mayer's putting a hold on my account till I turned in last week's dozen. Last week's dozen consisted of *The Philadelphia Story,* which I was only halfway through. So it was heigh-ho, heigh-ho, off to work we go to find twelve squeaky-cleans I could claim I'd already edited, and what better place to look than Disney?

Only *Snow White* had a cottage full of beer tankards and a dungeon full of wine goblets and deadly potions. *Sleeping Beauty* was no better—it had a splatted royal steward who'd drunk himself literally under the table—and *Pinocchio* not only drank beer but smoked cigars the Anti-Smoking League had somehow missed. Even *Dumbo* got drunk.

But animation wipes are comparatively easy, and all *Alice in Wonderland* had was a few smoke rings, so I was able to finish off the dozen and replenish *my* stock of deadly potions so at least I didn't have to watch *Fantasia* cold sober. And a good thing, too. The *Pastorale* sequence in *Fantasia* was so full of wine it took me five days to clean it up, after which I went back to

The Philadelphia Story and stared at Jimmy Stewart, trying to think of some way to salvage him, and then gave up and waited for my skids suspension to be over.

As soon as it was, I went out to Burbank to apologize to Alis, but more time must have gone by than I realized because there was a CG class cramming the unstacked chairs, and when I asked one of the hackates where Michael Caine and the film hist class had gone, he said, "That was last semester."

I stocked up on chooch and went to the next party and asked Heada for Alis's class schedule.

"I don't do chooch anymore," Heada said. She was wearing a tight sweater and skirt and black-framed glasses. *How to Marry a Millionaire.* "Why can't you leave her alone? She's not hurting anybody."

"I want—" I said, but I didn't know what I wanted. No, that wasn't true. What I wanted was to find a movie that didn't have a single AS in it. Only there weren't any.

"*The Ten Commandments,*" I said, back in my room again.

There was drinking in the golden-calf scene and assorted references to "the wine of violence," but it was better than *The Philadelphia Story*. I laid in a supply of grappa and asked for a list of biblical epics, and went to work playing Charlton Heston—deleting vineyards and calling a halt to Roman orgies. Vengeance is mine, saith the Lord.

SCENE: *Exterior of the Hardy house in summer. Picket fence, maple tree, flowers by front door. Slow dissolve to Autumn. Leaves falling. Tight focus on a leaf and follow it down.*

A-LA-LAND IS A LOT LIKE THE SKIDS. YOU STAND still and stare at a screen, or, worse, your own reflection, and after a while you're somewhere else.

The parties continued, packed with Marilyns and studio execs. Fred Astaire stayed in litigation, Heada avoided me, I drank. In excellent company. Gangsters drank, Navy lieutenants, little old ladies, sweet young things, doctors, lawyers, Indian chiefs. Fredric March, Jean Arthur, Spencer Tracy, Susan Hayward, Jimmy Stewart. And not just in *The Philadelphia Story*. The all-American, "shucks, wah-ah-all," do-the-honorable-thing boy next door got regularly splatted. Aquavit in *The Man Who Shot Liberty Valance*, brandy in *Bell, Book, and Candle*, "likker" straight from the jug in *How the West Was Won*. In *It's a Wonderful Life*, he got drunk enough to get thrown out of a bar and ran his car into a tree. In *Harvey,* he spent the entire film pleasantly tipsy, and what in hell was I supposed to do when I got to that movie? What in hell was I supposed to do in general?

Somewhere in there, Heada came to see me. "I've got a question," she said, standing in the door.

"Does this mean you're over being mad at me?" I said.

"Because you practically broke my arms? Because you thought the whole time you were popping me I was somebody else? What's to be mad about?"

"Heada . . ." I said.

"It's okay. Happens to me all the time. I should open a simsex parlor." She came in and sat down on the bunk. "I've got a question."

"I'll answer yours if you answer mine," I said.

"I don't know where she is."

"You know everything."

"She dropped out. The word is, she's working down on Hollywood Boulevard."

"Doing what?"

"I don't know. Probably not dancing in the movies, which should make you happy. You were always trying to talk her out of—"

I cut in with, "What's your question?"

"I watched that movie you told me I was playing a part in. *Rear Window?* Thelma Ritter? And all the meddling you said she did, telling him to mind his own business, telling him not to get involved. It was good advice. She was just trying to help."

"What's your question?"

"I watched this other movie. *Casablanca*. It's about this guy who has a bar in Africa someplace during World War II, and his old girlfriend shows up, only she's married to this other guy—"

"I know the plot," I said. "What part don't you understand?"

"All of it," she said. "Why the bar guy—"

"Humphrey Bogart," I said.

"Why Humphrey Bogart drinks all the time, why he says he won't help her and then he does, why he tells her she can't stay. If the two of them are so splatted about each other, why can't she stay?"

"There was a war on," I said. "They both had work to do."

"And this work was more important than the two of them?"

"Yeah," I said, but I didn't believe it, in spite of Rick's whole "hill of beans" speech. Ilsa's lending moral support to her husband, Rick's fighting in the Resistance weren't more important. They were a substitute. They were what you did when you couldn't have what you wanted. "The Nazis would get them," I said.

"Okay," she said doubtfully. "So they can't stay together. But why can't he still pop her before she leaves?"

"Standing there at the airport?"

"No," she said, very serious. "Before. Back at the bar."

Because he can't have her, I thought. And he knows it.

"Because of the Hays Office," I said.

"In real life she would have given him a pop."

"That's a comforting thought," I said. "But the movies aren't real life. And they can't tell you how people feel. They've got to show you. Valentino rolling his eyes, Rhett sweeping Scarlett off her feet, Lillian Gish clutching her heart. Bogie loves Ingrid and can't have her." I could see her looking blank again. "The bar owner loves his old girlfriend, so they have to *show* you by not letting him touch her or even give her a good-bye kiss. He has to just stand there and look at her."

"Like you drinking all the time and falling off the skids," she said.

Now it was my turn to look blank.

"The night Alis brought you back to my room, the night you were so splatted."

I still didn't get it.

"Showing the feelings," Heada said. "You trying to walk through the skids screen and nearly getting killed and Alis pulling you out."

SCENE: *Exterior. The Hardy house. Wind whirls the dead leaves. Slow dissolve to a bare-branched tree. Snow. Winter.*

I'd apparently had quite a night that night. I had tried to walk through the skids wall like a druggate on too much rave and then popped the wrong person. A wonderful performance, Andrew.

And Alis had saved me. I took the skids down to Hollywood Boulevard to look for her, checking at Screen Test City and at A Star Is Born, which had a River Phoenix lookalike working there. The Happy Endings booth had changed its name to Happily Ever After and was featuring *Dr. Zhivago,* Omar Sharif and Julie Christie in the field of flowers, smiling and holding a baby. A knot of half-interested tourates were watching it.

"I'm looking for a face," I said.

"Take your pick," the guy said. "Lara, Scarlett, Marilyn—"

"We were down here a few months ago," I said, trying to jog his memory. "We talked about *Casablanca*. . . ."

"I got *Casablanca,*" he said. "I got *Wuthering Heights, Love Story*—"

"This face," I interrupted. "She's about so high, light brown hair—"

"Freelancer?" he said.

"No," I said. "Never mind."

I walked on. There was nothing else on this side except VR caves. I stood there and thought about them, and about the simsex parlors farther down and the freelancers hustling out in front of them in torn net leotards, and then went back to Happily Ever After.

"*Casablanca,*" I said, pushing in front of the tourates, who'd decided to get in line. I slapped down my card.

The guy led me inside. "You got a happy ending for it?" he asked.

"You bet."

He sat me down in front of the comp, an ancient-looking Wang. "Now what you do is push this button, and your choices'll come up on the screen. Push the one you want. Good luck."

I rotated the airplane forty degrees, flattened it to two-dimensional, and made it look like the cardboard it had been. I'd never seen a fog machine. I settled for a steam engine, spewing out great belching puffs of cloud, and ff'd to the three-quarters' shot of Bogie telling Ingrid, "We'll always have Paris."

"Expand frame perimeter," I said, and started filling in their feet, Ingrid in flats and Bogie in lifts, big chunky blocks of wood strapped to his shoes with pieces of—

"What in hell do you think you're doing?" the guy said, bursting in.

"Just trying to inject a little reality into the proceedings," I said.

He shoved me out of the chair and started pushing keys. "Get out of here."

The tourates who'd been ahead of me were standing in front of the screen, and a little crowd had formed around them.

"The plane was cardboard and the airplane mechanics were midgets," I said. "Bogie was only five four. Fred Astaire was the son of an immigrant brewery worker. He only had a sixth-grade education."

The guy emerged from the booth steaming like my fog machine.

" 'Here's looking at you, kid' took seventeen takes," I said, heading toward the skids. "None of it's real. It's all done with mirrors."

SCENE: *Exterior. The Hardy house in winter. Dirty snow on roof, lawn, piled on either side of front walk. Slow dissolve to spring.*

I don't remember whether I went back down to Hollywood Boulevard again. I know I went to the parties, hoping Alis would show up in the doorway again, but not even Heada was there.

In between, I raped and pillaged and looked for something easy to fix. There wasn't anything. Sobering up the doctor in *Stagecoach* ruined the giving birth scene. *D.O.A.* went dead on arrival without Dana Andrews slugging back shots of whiskey, and *The Thin Man* disappeared altogether.

I called up the menu again, looking for something AS-free, something clean-cut and all-American. Like Alis's musicals.

"Musicals," I said, and the menu chopped itself into categories and put up a list. I scrolled through it.

Not *Carousel*. Billy Bigelow was a lush. So was Ava Gardner in *Showboat* and Van Johnson in *Brigadoon*. *Guys and Dolls?* No dice. Marlon Brando'd gotten a missionary splatted on rum. *Gigi?* It was full of liquor and cigars, not to mention "The Night They Invented Champagne."

Seven Brides for Seven Brothers? Maybe. It didn't have any saloon scenes or "Belly Up To The Bar, Boys" numbers. Maybe some

other Lesson, Andrew, in not mixing bourbon with *Rio Bravo* tequila.

"Beginning credits," I said, and went back and wiped the bottle in the boardinghouse scene and then triple-timed to the barnraising again to turn the jug into a pan of corn bread, and then thought I'd better watch the rest of the scene to make sure the jug wasn't visible in any of the other shots.

"Print and send," I said, "and forward realtime."

And there she was again. Dancing in the movies.

MOVIE CLICHE #15: The Hangover. (Usually follows #14: The Party.) Headache, jumping at loud noises, flinching at daylight.

SEE: *The Thin Man, The Tender Trap, After the Thin Man, McLintock!, Another Thin Man, The Philadelphia Story, Song of the Thin Man.*

I ACCESSED HEADA, NO VISUAL. "DO YOU know of anything that can sober me up?"

"Fast or painless?"

"Fast."

"Ridigaine," she said promptly. "What's up?"

"Nothing's up," I said. "Mayer's bugging me to work harder on his movies, and I decided the AS's are slowing me down. Do you have any?"

"I'll have to ask around," she said. "I'll get some and bring it over."

That's not necessary, I wanted to say, which would only make her more suspicious. "Thanks," I said.

While I was waiting for her I called up the credits. They weren't much help. There were seven brides, after all, and the only ones I knew were Jane Powell and Ruta Lee, who'd been in every B-picture made in the seventies. Dorcas was Julie Newmeyer, who'd later changed her name to Julie Newmar. When I went back and looked at the barnraising scene again, it was obvious which one she was.

I watched it, listening for the other characters' names. The little blonde Russ Tamblyn was in love with was named Alice, and Dorcas was the tall brunette. I ff'd to the kidnapping scene and matched the other girls to their characters' names. The one in the pink dress was Virginia Gibson.

Virginia Gibson. "Screen Actors' Guild directory," I said, and gave it the name.

Virginia Gibson had been in an assortment of movies, including *Athena* and something called *I Killed Wild Bill Hickok*.

"Musicals," I said, and the list shrank to five. No, four. *Funny Face* had Fred Astaire in it, which meant it was in litigation.

There was a knock on the door. I blanked the screen, then decided that would be a dead giveaway. "*Notorious*," I said, and then chickened out. What if Ingrid Bergman had Alis's face, too? "Cancel," I said, and tried to think of another movie, any movie. Except *Athena*.

"Tom, are you okay?" Heada called through the door.

"Coming," I said, staring at the blank screen. *Saratoga Trunk?* No, that had Ingrid in it, too, and anyway, if this was going to happen all the time, I'd better know it before I took anything else.

"*Notorious,*" I said softly, "Frame 54-119," and waited for Ingrid's face to come up.

"Tom!" Heada shouted. "Is something wrong?"

Cary Grant went out of the ballroom, and Ingrid gazed after him, looking anxious and like she was about to cry. And looking like Ingrid, which was a relief.

"Tom!" Heada said, and I opened the door.

Heada came in and handed me some blue capsules. "Take two. With water. Why didn't you answer the door?"

"I was getting rid of the evidence," I said, pointing at the screen. "Thirty-four champagne bottles."

"I watched that movie," she said, going over to the screen. "It's set in Brazil. It's got stock shots of Rio de Janeiro and Sugar Loaf."

"Right as always," I said, and then, casually, "Speaking of which, you know everything, Heada. Do you know if Fred Astaire's been copyrighted yet?"

"No," she said. "ILMGM's appealing."

"How long before these ridigaine take effect?" I said before she could ask why I wanted to know about Fred Astaire.

"Depends on how much you've got in your system," she said. "The way you've been popping it, six weeks."

"Six *weeks*?"

"I'm kidding," she said. "Four hours, maybe less. Are you sure you want to do this? What if you start flashing again?"

I didn't ask her how she knew I'd been flashing. This was, after all, Heada.

She handed me the glass. ''Drink lots of water. And pee as much as you can,'' she said. ''What's really up?''

''Slashing and burning,'' I said, turning back to the frozen screen. I cut out another champagne bottle.

She leaned over my shoulder. ''Is this the scene where they run out of champagne, and Claude Rains goes down to the wine cellar and catches Cary Grant?''

''Not when I get through with it,'' I said. ''The champagne's going to be ice cream. What do you think, should the uranium be hidden in the ice-cream freezer or the bag of rock salt?''

She looked at me seriously. ''I *think* there's something wrong. What is it?''

''I'm four weeks behind on Mayer's list, and he's twitching down my neck, that's what's wrong. Are you sure these are ridigaine?'' I said, peering at the capsules. ''They aren't marked.''

''I'm sure,'' she said, still looking suspiciously at me.

I popped the capsules in my mouth and reached for the bourbon.

Heada snatched it out of my hand. ''You take them with *water*.'' She went in the bathroom, and I could hear the gurgle of the bourbon being poured down the drain.

She came out of the bathroom and handed me a glass of water. ''Drink as much as you can. It'll help flush your system faster. No alcohol.'' She opened the closet, felt around inside, pulled out a bottle of vodka.

''*No* alcohol,'' she said, unscrewing the cap, and went back in the bathroom to pour it out. ''Any other bottles?''

"Why?" I said, sitting down on the bed. "You decide to switch over from chooch?"

"I told you, I quit," she said. "Stand up."

I did, and she knelt down and started fishing under the bed.

"Which is how I know how the ridigaine's going to make you feel," she said, pulling out a bottle of champagne. "You'll want a drink, but don't. You'll just toss it. And I mean toss it." She fumbled with the cork on the bottle. "So don't drink. And don't try to do anything. Lie down as soon as you start feeling anything, headache, shakes. And stay there. You might have halluces. Snakes, monsters . . . "

"Six-foot-tall rabbits named Harvey," I said.

"I'm not kidding," she said. "I felt like I was going to die when I took it. And chooch is a lot easier to quit than alcohol."

"So why'd you quit?" I said.

She gave me a wry look and went back to messing with the cork. "I thought it would make somebody notice me."

"And did they?"

"No," she said, and went back to messing with the cork. "Why did you call and ask me to bring you some ridigaine?"

"I told you," I said. "Mayer—"

She popped the cork. "Mayer's in New York, pimping support for his new boss, who, the word has it, is on the way out. The rumor is the ILMGM execs don't like his high-handed moralizing. At least when it applies to them." She poured out the champagne and came back in the room. "Any other champagne?"

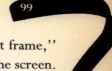

"Lots," I said, and went over to the comp. "Next frame," I said, and a tubful of champagne bottles came up on the screen. "You want to pour these out, too?" I turned, grinning.

She was looking at me seriously. "What's really up?"

"Next frame," I said. The screen shifted to Ingrid, looking anxious, her hair like a halo. I took the champagne glass out of her hand.

"You saw her again, didn't you?" she said.

Everything.

"Who?" I said, even though it was hopeless. "Yeah," I said. "I saw her." I shut off *Notorious*. "Come here," I said, "I want you to look at something."

"*Seven Brides for Seven Brothers*," I said to the comp. "Frame 25-118."

The screen lit Jane Powell, sitting in the wagon, holding a basket.

"Forward realtime," I said, and Jane Powell handed the basket to Julie Newmar.

"I thought this was going into litigation," Heada said over my shoulder.

"Over who?" I said. "Jane Powell or Howard Keel?"

"Russ Tamblyn," she said, pointing at him. He'd climbed on the wagon and was gazing soulfully at the little blonde, Alice. "Virtusonic's been using him in snuffporn movies, and ILMGM doesn't like it. They're claiming copyright abuse."

Russ Tamblyn, looking young and innocent, which was probably the point, went off with Alice, and Howard Keel lifted Jane Powell down off the buckboard.

"Stop," I said to the computer. "I want you to look at this next scene," I said to Heada. "At the faces. Forward realtime," I said, and the dancers formed two lines and bowed and curtsied to each other.

I don't know what I'd expected Heada to do—gasp and clutch her heart like Lillian Gish maybe. Or turn to me halfway through and ask, "What exactly is it I'm supposed to be looking for?"

She didn't do either. She watched the entire scene, still and silent, her face almost as focused on the screen as Alis's had been, and then said quietly, "I didn't think she'd do it."

For a moment I couldn't register what she said for the roaring in my head, the roaring that was saying, "It *is* her. It's not a flash. It *is* her."

"All that talk about finding a dance teacher," Heada was saying. "All that stuff about Fred Astaire. I never thought she'd—"

"Never thought she'd do what?" I said blankly.

"This," she said, waving her hand vaguely at the screen, where the sides of the barn were going up. "That she'd end up as somebody's popsy," she said. "That she'd sign on. Give up. Sell out." She gestured at the screen again. "Did Mayer say which of the studio execs you were doing it for?"

"I didn't do it," I said.

"Well, *somebody* did it," she said. "Mayer must've asked Vincent or somebody. I thought you said she didn't want her face pasted on somebody else's."

"She didn't. She doesn't," I said. "This isn't a paste-up. It's her, dancing."

She looked at the screen. A cowboy brought his hammer down hard on Russ Tamblyn's thumb.

"She wouldn't sell out," I said.

"To quote a friend of mine," she said, "everybody sells out."

"No," I said. "People sell out to get what they want. Getting her face pasted onto somebody else's body isn't what she wanted. She wanted to dance in the movies."

"Maybe she needed the money," Heada said, looking at the screen. Someone whacked Howard Keel with a board, and Russ Tamblyn took a poke at him.

"Maybe she figured out she couldn't have what she wanted."

"No," I said, thinking about her standing there on Hollywood Boulevard, her face set. "You don't understand. No."

"*Okay,*" she said placatingly. "She didn't sell out. It isn't a paste-up." She waved at the screen. "So what is it? How'd she get on there if somebody didn't paste her in?"

Howard Keel shoved a pair of brawlers into the corner, and the barn fell apart, collapsing into a clatter of boards and chagrin. "I don't know," I said.

We both stood there a minute, looking at the wreckage.

"Can I see the scene again?" Heada said.

"Frame 25-200, forward realtime," I said, and Howard Keel reached up again to lift Jane Powell down. The dancers formed their lines. And there was Alis, dancing in the movies.

"Maybe it isn't her," Heada said. "That's why you asked me to bring over the ridigaine, wasn't it, because you thought it might be the alcohol?"

"You see her, too."

"I know," she said, frowning, "but I'm not really sure I know what she looks like. I mean, the times I saw her I was pretty splatted, and so were you. And it wasn't all that many times, was it?"

That party, and the time Heada sent her to ask me for the access, and the episode of the skids. Memorable occasions, all.

"No," I said.

"So it could be it's just somebody else who looks like her. Her hair's darker than that, isn't it?"

"A wig," I said. "Wigs and makeup can make you look really different."

"Yeah," Heada said, as if that proved something. "Or really alike. Maybe this person's wearing a wig and makeup that makes her look like Alis. Who is it anyway? In the movie?"

"Virginia Gibson," I said.

"Maybe this Virginia Gibson and Alis just look alike. Was she in any other movies? Virginia Gibson, I mean? If she was, we could look at them and see what she looks like, and if this is her or not." She looked concernedly at me. "You'd better let the ridigaine work first, though. Are you having any symptoms yet? Headache?"

"No," I said, looking at the screen.

"Well, you will in a few minutes." She pulled the blankets off the bed. "Lie down, and I'll get you some water. Ridigaine's fast, but it's rough. The best thing is if you can—"

"Sleep it off," I said.

She brought a glass of water in and set it by the bed. "Access me if you get the shakes and start seeing things."

"According to you, I already am."

"I didn't *say* that. I just said you should check out this Virginia Gibson before you jump to any conclusions. *After* the ridigaine does its stuff."

"Meaning that when I'm sober, it won't look like her."

"Meaning that when you're sober, you'll at least be able to see her." She looked steadily at me. "Do you want it to be her?"

"I think I will lie down," I said to get her to leave. "My head aches." I sat down on the bed.

"It's starting to work," she said triumphantly. "*Access* me if you need anything."

"I will," I said, and lay back.

She looked around the room. "You don't have any more liquor in here, do you?"

"Gallons," I said, gesturing toward the screen. "Bottles, flasks, kegs, decanters. You name it, it's in there."

"It'll just make it worse if you drink anything."

"I know," I said, putting my hand over my eyes. "Shakes, pink elephants, six-foot-tall rabbits, 'and how are you, Mr. Wilson?' "

"*Access* me," she said, and left, finally.

I waited five minutes for her to come back and tell me to be sure and piss, and then another five for the snakes and rabbits to show up, or worse, Fred and Eleanor, dressed in white and dancing side by side. And thinking about what Heada'd said. If it wasn't a paste-up, what was it? And it couldn't be a paste-up. Heada hadn't heard Alis talking about wanting to dance in the movies. She hadn't seen her, that night down on Hollywood Boulevard, when I offered her a chance at one. She could have been digitized that night, been Ginger Rogers, Ann Miller, anybody she wanted. Even Eleanor Powell. Why would she have suddenly changed her mind and decided she wanted to be a dancer nobody'd ever heard of? An actress who'd only appeared in a handful of movies. One of which starred Fred Astaire.

"We're *this* close to having time travel," the exec had said, his thumb and finger almost touching.

And what if Alis, who was willing to do anything to dance in the movies, who was willing to practice in a cramped classroom with a tiny monitor and work nights in a tourate trap, had talked one of the time-travel hackates into letting her be a guinea pig? What if Alis had talked him into sending her back to 1954, dressed in a green weskit and short gloves, and then, instead of coming back like she was supposed to, had changed her name to Virginia Gibson and gone over to MGM to audition for a part in *Seven Brides for Seven Brothers*? And then gone on to be in six other movies. One of which was *Funny Face*. With Fred Astaire.

I sat up, slowly, so I wouldn't turn my headache into anything worse, and went over to the terminal and called up *Funny Face*.

Heada had said Fred Astaire was still in litigation, and he was. I put a watch-and-warn on both the movie and Fred in case the case got settled. If Heada was right—and when wasn't she?—Warner would turn around and file immediately, but if there was a glitch or Warner's lawyers were busy with Russ Tamblyn, there might be a window. I set the watch-and-warn to beep me and called up the list of Virginia Gibson's musicals again.

Starlift was a World War II b-and-w, which wouldn't give me as clear an image as color, and *She's Back on Broadway* was in litigation, too, for someone I'd never heard of. That left *Athena, Painting the Clouds with Sunshine,* and *Tea for Two,* none of which I could remember ever seeing.

When I called up *Athena,* I could see why. It was a cross between *One Touch of Venus* and *You Can't Take It with You,* with lots of floating chiffon and health-food eccentrics and almost no dancing. Virginia Gibson, in green chiffon, was supposed to be Niobe, the goddess of jazz and tap or something. Whatever she was, it wasn't Alis. It looked like her, especially with her hair pulled back in a Greek ponytail. "And with a fifth of bourbon in you," Heada would have said. And a double dose of ridigaine. Even then, it didn't look as much like her as the dancer in the barnraising scene. I called up *Seven Brides,* and the screen stayed silver for a long moment and then started scrolling legalese. "This movie currently in litigation and unavailable for viewing."

Well, that settled that. By the time the courts had decided to let Russ Tamblyn be sliced and diced, I'd be chooch free and able to see it was just somebody who looked like her, or not even that. A trick of lights and makeup.

And there was no point in slogging through any more musicals to drive the point home. Any resemblance was purely alcoholic, and I should do what Doc Heada said, lie down and wait for it to pass. And then go back to slicing and dicing myself. I should call up *Notorious* and get it over with.

"*Tea for Two,*" I said.

Tea was a Doris Day pic, and I wondered if she was on Alis's bad-dancer list. She deserved to be. She smirked her way toothily through a tap routine with Gene Nelson, set in a rehearsal hall Alis would have killed for, all floor space and mirrors and no stacks of desks. There was a terrible Latin version of "Crazy Rhythm," Gordon MacRae singing "I Only Have Eyes for You," and then Virginia Gibson's big number.

And there was no question of her being Alis. With her hair down, she didn't even look that much like her. Or else the ridigaine was kicking in.

The routine was Hollywood's idea of ballet, more chiffon and a lot of twirling around, not the kind of routine Alis would have bothered with. *If* she'd had ballet back in Meadowville, and not just jazz and tap, but she hadn't, and Virginia obviously had, so Alis wasn't Virginia, and I was sober, and it was back to the bottles.

"Forward 64," I said, and watched Doris smirk her way through the title number and an unnecessary reprise. The next number was a big production number. Virginia wasn't in it, and I started to ff again and then stopped.

"Rew to music cue," I said, and watched the production number, counting the frame numbers. A blond couple stepped forward, did a series of toe slides, and stepped back again, and a dark-haired guy and a redhead in a white pleated skirt kicked forward and went into a side-by-side Charleston. She had curly hair and a tied-in-front blouse, and the two of them put their hands on their knees and did a series of cross kicks. "Frame 75-004, forward 12," I said, and watched the routine in slow motion.

"Enhance quadrant 2," and watched the red hair fill the screen, even though there wasn't any need for an enhancement, or for the slowmo, either. No question at all of who it was.

I had known the instant I saw her, the same way I had in the barnraising scene, and it wasn't the booze (of which there was at least fifteen minutes' worth less in my system) or klieg, or a passing resemblance enhanced with rouge and eyebrow pencil. It was Alis. Which was impossible.

"Last frame," I said, but this was the Good Old Days when the chorus line didn't get into the credits, and the copyright date had to be deciphered. MCML. 1950.

I went back through the movie, going to freeze frame and enhance every time I spotted red hair, but I didn't see her again. I ff'd to the Charleston number and watched it again, trying to come up with a theory.

Okay. The hackate had sent her to 1950 (scratch that—the copyright was for the release date—had sent her to 1949) and she had waited around for four years, dancing chorus parts and palling around with Virginia Gibson, waiting for her chance to clunk Virginia on the head, stuff her behind a set, and take her place in *Brides*. So she could impress the producer of *Funny Face* with her dancing so that he'd offer her a part, and she'd finally get to dance with Fred, if only in the same production number.

Even splatted on chooch, I couldn't have bought that one. But it was her, so there had to be an explanation. Maybe in between chorus jobs Alis had gotten a job as a warmbody. They'd had them back then. They were called stand-ins, and maybe she got to be Virginia Gibson's because they looked alike, and Alis had bribed her to let her take her place, just for one number, or had connived to have Virginia miss a shooting session. Anne Baxter in *All About Eve*. Or maybe Virginia had an AS problem, and when she'd showed up drunk, Alis had had to take her place.

That theory wasn't much better. I called up the menu again. If Alis had gotten one chorus job, she might have gotten others. I scanned through the musicals, trying to remember which ones had chorus numbers. *Singin' in the Rain* did. That party scene I'd taken all that champagne out of.

I called up the record of changes to find the frame number and ff'd through the nonchampagne, to Donald O'Connor's saying, "You gotta show a movie at a party. It's a Hollywood law," through said movie, to the start of the chorus number.

Girls in skimpy pink skirts and flapper hats ran onstage to the tune of "You Are My Lucky Star" and a bad camera angle. I was going to have to do an enhance to see their faces clearly. But there wasn't any need to. I'd found Alis.

And she might have managed to bribe Virginia Gibson. She might even have managed to stuff her and the *Tea for Two* redhead behind their respective sets. But Debbie Reynolds hadn't had an AS problem, and if Alis had crammed her behind a set, *somebody* would have noticed.

It wasn't time travel. It was something else, a comp-generated illusion of some kind in which she'd somehow managed to dance and get it on film. In which case, she hadn't disappeared forever into the past. She was still in Hollywood. And I was going to find her.

"Off," I said to the comp, grabbed my jacket, and flung myself out the door.

**MOVIE CLICHE #419: The Blocked Escape.
Hero/Heroine on the run, near escape with
bad guys, eludes them, nearly home free, villain looms up suddenly, asks, "Going somewhere?"**

SEE: *The Great Escape, The Empire Strikes Back,
North by Northwest, The Thirty-Nine Steps.*

EADA WAS STANDING OUTSIDE THE DOOR, ARMS folded, tapping her foot. Rosalind Russell as the Mother Superior in *The Trouble with Angels.*

"You're supposed to be lying down," she said.

"I feel fine."

"That's because the alcohol isn't out of your system yet," she said. "Sometimes it takes longer than others. Have you peed?"

"Yes," I said. "Buckets. Now if you'll excuse me, Nurse Ratchet . . ."

"Wherever you're going, it can wait till you're clean," she

110

said, blocking my way. "I mean it. Ridigaine's not anything to fool with." She steered me back into the room. "You need to stay here and rest. Where were you going anyway? To see Alis? Because if you were, she's not there. She's dropped all her classes and moved out of her dorm."

And in with Mayer's boss, she meant. "I wasn't going to see Alis."

"Where *were* you going?"

It was useless to lie to Heada, but I tried it anyway. "Virginia Gibson was in *Funny Face*. I was going out to try to find a copy of it."

"Why can't you get it off the fibe-op?"

"Fred Astaire's in it. That's why I asked you if he was out of litigation." I let that sink in for a couple of frames. "You said it might just be a likeness. I wanted to see if it's Alis or just somebody who looks like her."

"So you were going out to look for a pirated copy?" Heada said, as if she almost believed me. "I thought you said she was in six musicals. They aren't all in litigation, are they?"

"There weren't any close-ups in *Athena*," I said, and hoped she wouldn't ask why I couldn't enhance. "And you know how she is about Fred Astaire. If she's going to be in anything, it'd be *Funny Face*."

None of this made any sense, since the idea was supposedly to find something Virginia Gibson was in, not Alis, but Heada nodded when I mentioned Fred Astaire. "I can get you one," she said.

"Thanks," I said. "It doesn't even have to be digitized.

Tape'll work." I led her to the door. "I'll stay here and lie down and let the ridigaine do its stuff."

She crossed her arms again.

"I swear," I said. "I'll give you my key. You can lock me in."

"You'll lie down?"

"Promise," I lied.

"You won't," she said, "and you'll wish you had." She sighed. "At least you won't be on the skids. Give me the key."

I handed her the card.

"Both of them," she said.

I handed her the other card.

"Lie *down*," she said, and shut the door and locked me in.

"It's easier to do a scratch construct," he said, looking at the screen where Clint was standing, waiting for orders. "Or a paste-up. What kind of liveaction? Human?"

"Yeah, human," I said, "but a paste-up won't work. So how do I bluescreen it in?"

He shrugged. "Set up a pixar and compositor. Maybe an old Digimatte, if you can find one. The tourate traps use them sometimes. The hard part's the patching—lights, perspective, camera angles, edges."

I'd stopped listening. The A Star Is Born place down on Hollywood Boulevard had had a Digimatte. And Heada'd said Alis had gotten a job down there.

"It still won't be as good as a graphic," he was saying. "But if you've got an expert melder, it's possible."

And a pixar, *and* the comp know-how, *and* the accesses. None of which Alis had. "What if you didn't have accesses? Say you wanted to do it without anyone knowing about it?"

"I thought you had full studio access," he said, suddenly interested. "Did Mayer fire you?"

"This is *for* Mayer. I'm taking the AS's out of a hackate movie," I said glibly. "*Rising Sun*. There are too many visual references to do a wipe. I've got to do a whole new scene, and I want it to be authentic."

I was counting on his not having seen the movie, or knowing it was made before accesses, a good bet with somebody who'd turn Clint Eastwood into a marionette. "The hero superimposes a fake image over a real one. To catch a criminal."

He was frowning vaguely. "Somebody breaks into the fibe-op feed in this movie?"

"Yeah," I said. "So how do I make it look like the real thing?"

"Source piracy? You don't," he said. "You have to have studio access."

Nowhere fast. "I don't have to show anything illegal," I said, "just talk about how he finds a bypass around the encryptions or breaks into the authorization guards," but he was already shaking his head.

"It doesn't work like that," he said. "The studios have paid too much for their properties and actors to let source piracy happen, and encryptions, authorization guards, navajos, all those can be gotten around. That's why they went to the fibe-op loop. What goes out comes back in."

Up on the screen Clint had started moving. I glanced up. He was walking in a figure-eight pattern, hands down, head down. Looping.

"The fibe-op feed sends the signal out and back again in a continuous loop. It's got an ID-lock built in. The lock matches the signal coming in against the one that went out, and if they don't match, it rejects the incoming and substitutes the old one."

"Every frame?" I said, thinking maybe the lock only checked every five minutes, enough time to squeeze in a dance routine.

"Every frame."

"Doesn't that take a ton of memory? A pixel-by-pixel match?"

"Brownian check," he said, but that wasn't much better. The lock would check random pixels and see if they matched, and there'd be no way to know in advance which ones. The only thing you'd be able to change the image to was another one exactly like it.

"What about when you have accesses?" I said, watching Clint make the circuit, around and around. Boris Karloff in *Frankenstein*.

"In that case, the lock checks the altered image for authorization and then allows it past."

"And there's no way to get a fake access?" I said.

He was looking at the screen irritatedly, as if I was the one who'd set Frankenstein in motion. "Sit," he said. Clint sat.

"Stay," I said.

Vincent glared at me. "What movie did you say this was for?"

"A remake," I said, looking over at the door. Heada was coming in. "Maybe I'll just stay with the wipe," I said, and ducked off toward the stairs.

"I still don't see why you insist on doing it by hand," he called after me. "There's no point. I've got a search-and-destroy program—"

I skidded upstairs and punched in the override, cursing myself for locking the door in the first place, opened it, got in bed, remembered the door was supposed to be locked, locked it, and flung myself back on the bed.

Hurrying had not been a good idea. My head had started to pound like the drums in the Latin number in *Tea for Two*.

I closed my eyes and waited for Heada, but it must not have been her in the doorway, or else she had gotten waylaid by Vincent and his dancing dolls. I called up *Three Sailors and a Girl,* but all the "next, please" 's made me faintly seasick. I closed my eyes, waiting for the queasiness to pass, and then opened them again and tried to come up with a theory that didn't belong in a movie.

Alis couldn't have bluescreened herself in like Gene Kelly's mouse. She didn't know anything about comps—she'd been taking Basic CG 101 last fall when I got her class schedule out of Heada. And even if she had somehow mastered melds and shading and rotoscoping, she still didn't have the accesses.

Maybe she'd gotten somebody to help her. But who? The undergrad hackates didn't have accesses either, and Vincent wouldn't have understood why she insisted on doing it by hand.

So it had to be a paste-up. And why not? Maybe Alis had finally realized dancing in the movies was impossible, or maybe Mayer'd promised to find her a dancing teacher if she'd pop his boss. She wouldn't be the first face to come to Hollywood and end up on a casting couch.

But if that were the case, she wouldn't have looked like she did. I called up *On the Town* again and peered at it through my headache. Alis leaped lightly around the Empire State Building, animated and happy. I turned it off and tried to sleep.

If it was a paste-up, she wouldn't have had that focused, intent look. Vincent, programs or no programs, could never have captured that smile.

Slow pan from comp screen to clock, showing 11:05, and back to screen. Shot of sailors dancing. Slow pan to clock, showing 3:45.

S OMEWHERE IN THE MIDDLE OF THE NIGHT IT occurred to me that there was another reason Mayer couldn't have done a paste-up of Alis. The best reason of all: Heada didn't know about it.

She knew everything, every bit and piece of popsy, every studio move, every takeover rumor. There wasn't anything that got by her. If Alis had given in to Mayer, Heada would have known about it before it happened. And reported it to me, as if it was what I wanted to hear.

And wasn't it? I had told Alis she couldn't have what she wanted, that dancing in the movies was impossible, and it was a paste-up or nothing, and everybody likes to be proved right, don't they?

Especially if they are right. You can't just walk through a movie screen like Mia Farrow in *The Purple Rose of Cairo* and take Virginia Gibson's place. You can't just walk through a looking glass like Charlotte Henry and find yourself dancing with Fred Astaire.

Even if that's what it looks like you're doing. It's a trick of lighting, that's all, and makeup, and too much liquor, too much klieg; and the only cure for that was to follow Heada's orders, piss, drink lots of water, try to sleep.

"*Three Sailors and a Girl,*" I said, and waited for the trick to be revealed.

Slow pan from comp screen to clock, showing 4:58, and back to screen. Shot of sailors dancing. Slow pan to clock, showing 7:22.

EELING BETTER?'' HEADA SAID. SHE WAS SIT-
ting on the bed, holding a glass of water. ''I
told you ridigaine was rough.''

''Yeah,'' I said, closing my eyes against the
glare from the glass.

''Drink this,'' she said, and stuck a straw in
my mouth. ''How's the craving? Bad?''

I didn't want to drink anything, including water. ''No.''

''You sure?'' she said suspiciously.

''I'm sure,'' I said. I opened my eyes again, and when that
went okay, I tried to sit up. ''What took you so long?''

''After I found *Funny Face,* I went and talked to one of the
ILMGM execs. You were right about it's not being Mayer. He's
sworn off popsy. He's trying to convince Arthurton he's straight
and narrow.''

She stuck the straw under my nose again. "I talked to one of the hackates, too. He says there's no way to get liveaction stuff onto the fibe-op source without studio access. He says there are all kinds of securities and privacies and encryptions. He says there are so many, nobody, not even the best hackates, can get past them."

"I know," I said, leaning my head back against the wall. "It's impossible."

"Do you feel good enough to look at the disk?"

I didn't, and there was no point, but Heada put it in and we watched Fred dance circles around Audrey Hepburn and Paris.

The ridigaine was good for something, anyway. Fred was doing a series of swing turns, his feet tapping easily, carelessly, his arms extended, but there wasn't a quiver of a flash or even a soft-focus. My head still ached, but the drumming was gone, replaced by a bleak silence that felt like the aftermath of a flash and had its sharp clarity, its certainty.

I was certain Alis wouldn't have danced in this movie, with its modern dance and its duets, carefully choreographed by Fred to make Audrey Hepburn look like a better dancer than she was. Certain that when Virginia Gibson appeared, she'd be Virginia Gibson, who looked a lot like Alis.

And certain that when I called up *On the Town* and *Tea for Two* and *Singin' in the Rain,* it would still be Alis, no matter how secure the fibe-op loops, no matter how impossible.

Virginia Gibson came on in a gaggle of Hollywood's idea of fashion designers. "You don't see her, do you?" Heada said anxiously.

"No," I said, watching Fred.

"This Virginia Gibson person really does look a lot like Alis," Heada said. "Do you want to try *Seven Brides for Seven Brothers* again, just to make sure?"

"I'm sure," I said.

"Good," she said, standing up briskly. "Now, the main thing now that you're clean is to keep busy so you won't think about the craving, and anyway, you need to catch up on Mayer's list before he gets back, and I was thinking maybe I could help you. I've been watching a lot of movies, and I could tell you which ones have AS's in them and where it is. *The Color Purple* has a roadhouse scene where—"

"Heada," I said.

"And *after* you finish the list, maybe you and I could get Mayer to assign us a real remake. I mean, now that we're both clean. You said one time I'd make a great location assistant, and I've been watching a lot of movies. We'd make a great team. You could do the CGs—"

"I need you to do something for me," I said. "There was an ILMGM exec who used to come to the parties who was always using time travel as a line. I need you to find out his name."

"Time travel?" Heada said blankly.

"He said they were *this* close to discovering time travel," I said. "He kept talking about parallel timefeeds."

"You said it wasn't her in *Funny Face*," she said slowly.

"He kept talking about doing a remake of *Time After Time*."

She said, still blankly, "You think Alis went back in time?"

"I don't *know*," I said, and the last word was a shout. "Maybe she found a pair of ruby slippers, maybe she walked up onto the screen like Buster Keaton in *Sherlock Holmes, Jr.* I don't *know*!"

Heada was looking at me, her eyes full of tears. "But you're going to keep looking for her, aren't you? Even though it's impossible," she said bitterly. "Just like John Wayne in *The Searchers*."

"And he found Natalie Wood, didn't he?" I said. "Didn't he?" but she was already gone.

MONTAGE: *No sound.* **HERO,** *seated at comp, chin on hand, saying, "Next, please," as routine on screen changes. Hula, Latin number, clambake, Hollywood's idea of ballet, hobo number, water ballet, doll dance.*

I DIDN'T HAVE ALL THE ALCOHOL OUT OF MY system yet. Half an hour after Heada left, my headache came back with a vengeance. I called up *Two Sailors and a Girl* (or was it *Two Girls and a Sailor?*) and slept for two days straight.

When I got up, I pissed several gallons and then checked to see if Heada had accessed me. She hadn't. I tried to access her, and then Vincent, and started through the movies again.

Alis was in *I Love Melvin,* playing, natch, a chorus girl trying to break into the movies, and in *Let's Dance* and *Two Weeks with Love.* I found her in two Vera-Ellen movies, which I watched twice, convinced that I was somehow missing an important clue, and in *Painting the Clouds with Sunshine,* taking Virginia Gibson's

127

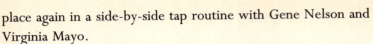

place again in a side-by-side tap routine with Gene Nelson and Virginia Mayo.

I accessed Vincent and asked him about parallel timefeeds. "Is this for *Rising Sun*?" he asked suspiciously.

"*The Time Machine*," I said. "Paul Newman and Julia Roberts. What *is* a parallel timefeed?" and got an earful of probability and causality and side-by-side universes.

"Every event has a dozen, a hundred, a thousand possible outcomes," he said. "The theory is there's a universe in which every single outcome actually exists."

A universe in which Alis gets to dance in the movies, I thought. A universe in which Fred Astaire's still alive and the CG revolution never happened.

I had been looking exclusively through musicals made during the fifties. But if there were parallel timefeeds, and Alis had somehow found a way to get in and out of those other universes, there was no reason she couldn't be in movies made later. Or earlier.

I started through the Busby Berkeleys, short as they were on dancing, and found her tapping without music in *Gold Diggers of 1935* and in the big finale of *42nd Street*, but that was it. I did better (and apparently so had she) in non-Busbys. *Hats Off*, wearing a hat, natch, and *Show of Shows* and *Too Much Harmony*, "Buckin' the Wind" in a number made for Marilyn, in garters and a white skirt that blew up around her stockinged legs. She was in *Born to Dance*, too, but in the chorus, and I couldn't find her in any other Eleanor Powell movies.

It took me a week to finish the b-and-w's, during which time

I couldn't get through to Heada, and she didn't access me. When my comp finally did beep, I didn't wait for her to come on. "Did you find out anything?" I said.

"I found out all right!" Mayer said, twitching. "You haven't sent in a movie in three weeks! I was planning to give the whole package to my boss at next week's meeting, and you're wasting time with *Rising Sun,* which isn't even on the list!"

Which meant Vincent was costarring in the role of Joe Spinell as snitch in *The Godfather II.*

"I needed to replace a couple of scenes," I said. "There were too many visuals to do wipes. One of them's a dance number. You don't know anybody who can dance, do you?" I watched him, looking for some sign, some indication that he remembered Alis, knew her, had wanted to pop her badly enough that he'd pasted her face in over a dozen dancers'. Nothing. Not even a pause in the twitches.

"There was a face at a couple of the parties a while back," I said. "Pretty, light brown hair, she wanted to dance in the movies."

Nothing. It wasn't Mayer.

"Forget dancers," he said. "Forget *The Time Machine.* Just take the damned alcohol *out!* I want the rest of that list done by Monday, or you'll never work for ILMGM again!"

"You can count on me, Mr. Potter," I said, and let him tell me he was shutting down my credit.

"I want you sober!" he said.

Which, oddly enough, I was.

I took "Moonshine Lullaby" out of *Annie Get Your Gun* and

the hookahs out of *Kismet* to show him I'd been listening, and started through the forties, looking for alcohol and Alis, two birds with one ff. She was in *Yankee Doodle Dandy,* and in the hoedown number in *Babes on Broadway,* wearing the pinafore she'd had on the night she'd come to ask me for the disk.

Heada came in while I was watching *Three Little Girls in Blue,* which had an assortment of bustles and Vera-Ellen, but no Alis.

"I found the exec," she said. "He's working for Warner now. He says they're looking at ILMGM as a possible take-over."

"What's his name?" I said.

"He wouldn't tell me anything. He said the reason they haven't rereleased *Somewhere in Time* is because they couldn't decide whether to cast Vivien Leigh or Marilyn Monroe."

"I'll talk to him. What's his name?"

She hesitated. "I talked to the hackates, too. They said last year they were transmitting images through a negative-matter region and got some interference that they thought was a time discrepancy, but they haven't been able to duplicate the results, and now they think it was a transmission from another source."

"How big of a time discrepancy?" I said.

She looked unhappy. "I asked them if they could duplicate the results, could they send a person back into the past, and they said even if it worked, they were only talking about elec-trons, not atoms, and there was no way anything living could survive a negative-matter region."

worse to come because Heada was still hovering by the door like Clara Bow in *Wings,* unwilling to tell me the bad news.

"Have you found her in any more movies?" she said.

"Six," I said. "And if it's not time travel, she must have walked up onto the screen like Mia Farrow. Because it's not a paste-up. And it's not Mayer."

"There's another explanation," she said unhappily. "You were pretty splatted there for a while. One of the movies I watched was about a guy who was an alcoholic."

"*Lost Weekend,*" I said. "Ray Milland," and could already see where this was going.

"He had blackouts when he drank," she said. "He did things and couldn't remember them." She looked at me. "You knew what she looked like. And you had the accesses."

DANA ANDREWS: [*Standing over police sergeant's desk*] She didn't do it, I tell you.
BRODERICK CRAWFORD: Is that so? Then who did?
DANA ANDREWS: I don't know, but I know she couldn't have. She's not that kind of girl.
BRODERICK CRAWFORD: Well, somebody did it. [*Eyes narrowing suspiciously*] Maybe you did it. Where were you when Carson was killed?
DANA ANDREWS: I was out taking a walk.

I T WAS THE LIKELIEST EXPLANATION. I WAS AN expert at paste-ups. And I'd had her face stuck in my head ever since the moment I flashed. And I had full studio access. Motive and opportunity.

I had wanted her, and she had wanted to dance in the movies, and in the wonderful world of CGs, anything is possible. But if I had done it, I

132

wouldn't have given her a two-minute bit in a production number. I'd have deleted Doris Day and her teeth and let Alis dance with Gene Nelson in front of those rehearsal-hall mirrors. If I'd known about the routine, which I hadn't. I'd never even seen *Tea for Two*.

Or I didn't *remember* seeing it. Right after the episode on the skids, Mayer had credited my account for half a dozen Westerns, none of which I remembered doing. But if I had done it, I wouldn't have dressed her in a bustle. I wouldn't have made her dance with Gene Kelly.

I'd put a watch-and-warn on Fred Astaire and *Funny Face*. I changed it to *Broadway Melody of 1940* and asked for a status report on the case. It was close to being settled, but a secondary suit was expected to be filed, and the FPS was considering proceedings.

The Film Preservation Society. Every change was automatically recorded with them, and the studios didn't have any control over them. Mayer hadn't been able to get me out of putting in those codes because they were part and parcel of the fibe-op feed. If it was a paste-up it would have to be listed in their records.

I called up the FPS's files and asked for the record for *Brides*.

Legalese. I'd forgotten it was in litigation. "*Singin' in the Rain*," I said.

The champagne wipes I'd done in the party scene were listed, along with one I hadn't. "Frame 9-106," it read, and listed the coordinates and the data. Jean Hagen's cigarette holder. It had been done by the Anti-Smoking League.

"*Tea for Two,*" I said, and tried to remember the frame numbers for the Charleston scene, but it didn't matter. The screen was empty.

Which left time travel. I went back to doing the musicals, saying, "Next, please!" to conga lines and male choruses and a horrible blackface number I was surprised nobody'd wiped before this. She was in *Can-Can* and *Bells Are Ringing,* both made in 1960, after which I didn't expect to find much. Musicals had gone big-budget around then, which meant buying up Broadway shows and casting box-office properties like Audrey Hepburn and Richard Harris in them who couldn't sing or dance, and then cutting out all the musical numbers to conceal the fact. And then musicals'd turned socially relevant. As if the coffin had needed any more nails pounded into it.

There was plenty of alcohol in the musicals of the sixties and seventies, though, even if there wasn't much dancing. A gin-soaked father in *My Fair Lady,* a gin-soaked popsy in *Oliver,* an entire gin-soaked mining camp in *Paint Your Wagon.* Also saloons, beer, whiskey, red-eye, and a falling-down-drunk Lee Marvin (who couldn't sing or dance, but then neither could Clint Eastwood or Jean Seberg, and who cares? There's always dubbing). The gin-soaked twenties in Lucille Ball's (who couldn't act either, a triple threat) *Mame.*

And Alis, dancing in the chorus in *Goodbye, Mr. Chips* and *The Boyfriend.* Doing the Tapioca in *Thoroughly Modern Millie,* high-stepping to "Put on Your Sunday Clothes" in *Hello Dolly!* in a sky-blue bustled dress and parasol.

I went out to Burbank. And maybe time travel was possible. At least two semesters had gone by, but the class was still there. And Michael Caine was still giving the same lecture.

"Any number of reasons have been advanced for the demise of the musical," he was intoning, "escalating production costs, widescreen technological complications, unimaginative staging. But the real reason lies deeper."

I stood against the door and listened to him give the eulogy while the class took respectful notes on their palmtops.

"The death of the musical was due not to directorial and casting catastrophes, but to natural causes. The world the musical depicted simply no longer existed."

The monitor Alis had used to practice with was still there, and so were the stacked-up chairs, only now there were a lot more of them. Michael Caine and the class were crammed into a space too narrow for a soft-shoe, and the chairs had been there awhile. They were covered with dust.

"The musical of the fifties depicted a world of innocent hopes and harmless desires." He muttered something to the comp, and Julie Andrews appeared, sitting on an Alpine hillside with a guitar and assorted children. An odd choice for his argument of "simpler times," since the movie'd been made in 1965, the year of the Vietnam buildup. Not to mention its being set in 1939, the year of the Nazis.

"It was a sunnier, less complicated time," he said, "a time when happy endings were still believable."

The screen skipped to Vanessa Redgrave and Franco Nero, surrounded by soldiers with torches and swords. *Camelot*. "That idyllic world died, and with it died the Hollywood musical, never to be resurrected.''

I waited till the class was gone and he'd had his snort of flake and asked him if he knew where Alis was, even though I knew it was no use, he wouldn't have helped her, and the last thing Alis would have needed was somebody else to tell her the musical was dead.

He didn't remember her, even after I'd plied him with chooch, and he refused to give me the student list for her class. I could get it from Heada, but I didn't want her looking sympathetic and thinking I'd lost my mind. Charles Boyer in *Gaslight.*

I went back to my room and took Billy Bigelow's drinking and half the plot out of *Carousel,* and went to bed.

An hour later the comp woke me out of a sound sleep, making a racket like the reactor in *The China Syndrome,* and I staggered over and blinked at it for a good five minutes before I realized it was the watch-and-warn, and *Brides* must be out of litigation, and another minute to think what command to give.

It wasn't *Brides.* It was Fred Astaire, and the court decision was scrolling down the screen: ''Intellectual property claim denied, irreproducible art form claim denied, collaborative property claim denied.'' Which mean Fred's estate and RKO-Warner must have lost, and ILMGM, where Fred had spent all those years covering for partners who couldn't dance, had won.

''*Broadway Melody of 1940,*'' I said, and watched the Beguine come up just like I remembered it, stars and polished floor and Eleanor in white, side by side with Fred.

I had never watched it sober. I had thought the silence, the raptness, the quality of still, centered beauty was the effect of the klieg, but it wasn't. They tapped easily, carelessly, across a dark, polished floor, their hands not quite touching, and were as still, as silent as they were that night I watched Alis watching them. The real thing.

And it had never existed, that harmless, innocent world. In 1940, Hitler was bombing the hell out of London and already hauling Jews off in cattle cars. The studio execs were lobbying against war and making deals, the real Mayer was running the studio, and starlets were going pop on a casting couch for a five-second walk-on. Fred and Eleanor were doing fifty takes, a hundred, in a hot airless studio, and going home to soak their bleeding feet.

It had never existed, this world of starry floors and backlit hair and easy, careless kick-turns, and the 1940 audience watching it knew it didn't. And that was its appeal, not that it reflected "sunnier, simpler times," but that it was impossible. That it was what they wanted and could never have.

The screen cut to legalese again, ILMGM's appeal already under way, and I hadn't seen the end of the routine, hadn't gotten it on tape or even backed it up.

It didn't matter. It was Eleanor, not Alis, and no matter what Heada thought, no matter how logical it was, I wasn't the one doing it. Because if I had been, litigation or no litigation, that was where I would have put her, dancing side by side with Fred, half turning to give him that delighted smile.

MONTAGE: *Tight close-up comp screen. Title credits dissolve into one another:* **South Pacific, Stand Up and Cheer, State Fair, Strike Up the Band, Summer Stock.**

E VENTUALLY I RAN OUT OF PLACES TO LOOK. I went down to Hollywood Boulevard again, but nobody remembered her, and none of the places had Digimattes except A Star Is Born, and it was closed for the night, an iron gate pulled across the front. Alis's other classes had been fibe-op-feed lectures, and her roommate, very splatted, was under the impression Alis had gone back home.

"She packed up all her stuff," she said. "She had all this stuff, costumes and wigs and stuff, and left."

"How long ago?"

"I don't know. Last week, I think. Before Christmas."

I talked to the roommate five weeks after I'd seen Alis in *Brides*. At the end of six weeks, I ran out of musicals. There weren't that many, and I'd watched them all, except for the ones in litigation because of Fred. And Ray Bolger, who Viamount filed copyright on the day after I went out to Burbank.

The Russ Tamblyn suit got settled, beeping me awake in the middle of the night to tell me somebody'd won the right to rape and pillage him on the big screen, and I backed up the barnraising scene and then watched *West Side Story,* just in case. Alis wasn't there.

I watched the ''On the Town'' routine again and looked up *Painting the Clouds with Sunshine,* convinced there was something important there that I was missing. It was a remake of *Gold Diggers of 1933,* but that wasn't what was bothering me. I put all the routines up on the array in order, easiest to most difficult, as if that might give me some clue to what she'd do next, but it wasn't any help. *Seven Brides for Seven Brothers* was the hardest thing she'd done, and she'd done that six weeks ago.

I listed the movies by date, studio, and dancers, and ran a cross-tabulation on the data. And then I sat and stared at the nonresults for a while. And at the array.

There was a knock on the door. Mayer. I blanked the screen and tried to think of a nonmusical to call up, but my mind had gone blank. ''*Philadelphia Story,*'' I said finally. ''Frame 115-010,'' and yelled, ''Come on in.''

It was Heada. ''I came to tell you Mayer's going nuclear about your not sending any movies,'' she said, looking at the screen. It was the wedding scene. Everybody, Jimmy Stewart, Cary Grant, were gathered around Katharine Hepburn, who had a huge hat and a hangover.

"The word is Arthurton's bringing in a new guy, supposedly to head up Editing," Heada said, "but really to be his assistant, in which case Mayer's out."

Good, I thought, at least that'll put a stop to the carnage. But if Mayer got fired, I'd lose my access, and I'd never find Alis.

"I'm working on them right now," I said, and launched into an elaborate explanation of why I was still on *Philadelphia Story*.

"Mayer offered me a job," Heada said.

"So now that he's hired you as a warmbody, you've got a stake in his not getting fired, and you've come to tell me to get busy?"

"No," she said. "Not warmbody. Location assistant. I leave for New York this afternoon."

It was the last thing I expected. I looked over at her and saw she was wearing a blazer and skirt. Heada as studio exec.

"You're leaving?" I said blankly.

"This afternoon," she said. "I came to give you my access number." She took out a hardcopy. "It's asterisk nine two period eight three three," she said, and handed me the piece of paper.

I looked at it, expecting the number, but it was a list of movie titles.

"None of them have any drinking in them," she said. "There are about three weeks' worth. They should stall Mayer for a while."

"Thank you," I said wonderingly.

"Betsy Booth strikes again," she said.

I must have looked blank.

"Judy Garland. *Love Finds Andy Hardy,*" she said. "I told you I've been watching a lot of movies. That's why I got the job. Location assistant has to know all the sets and stock shots and props and be able to find them for the hackate so he doesn't have to digitize new ones. It saves memory."

She pointed at the screen. "*The Philadelphia Story*'s got a public library, a newspaper office, a swimming pool, and a 1936 Packard." She smiled. "Remember when you said the movies taught us how to act and gave us lines to say? You were right. But you were wrong about which part I was playing. You said it was Thelma Ritter, but it wasn't." She waved her hand at the screen, where the wedding party was assembled. "It was Liz."

I frowned at the screen, unable for a moment to remember who Liz was. Katharine Hepburn's precocious little sister? No, wait. The other reporter, Jimmy Stewart's long-suffering girlfriend.

"I've been playing Joan Blondell," Heada said. "Mary Stuart Masterson, Ann Sothern. The girl next door, the secretary who's in love with her boss, only he never notices her, he thinks she's just a kid. He's in love with Tracy Lord, but Joan Blondell helps him anyway. She'd do anything for him, even watch movies."

She stuck her hands in her blazer pockets, and I wondered when she had stopped wearing the halter dress and the pink satin gloves.

"The secretary stands by him," Heada said. "She picks

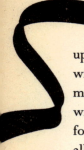

up after him and gives him advice. She even helps him out
with his romances, because she knows at the end of the
movie, he'll finally notice her, he'll realize he can't get along
without her, he'll figure out Katharine Hepburn's all wrong
for him and the secretary's the one he's been in love with
all along." She looked up at me. "But this isn't the movies,
is it?" she said bleakly.

Her hair wasn't platinum blonde anymore. It was light brown
with highlights in it. "Heada," I said.

"It's okay," she said. "I already figured that out. It's what
comes of taking too much klieg." She smiled. "In real life, Liz
would have to get over Jimmy Stewart, settle for being friends.
Audition for a new part. Joan Crawford maybe?"

I shook my head. "Rosalind Russell."

"Well, Melanie Griffith anyway," she said. "So, anyway, I
leave this afternoon, and I just wanted to say good-bye and have
you wish me luck."

"You'll be great," I said. "You'll own ILMGM in six
months." I kissed her on the cheek. "You know everything."

"Yeah."

She started out the door. " 'Here's lookin' at you, kid,' "
she said.

I watched her down the hall, and then went back in the room,
looking at the list Heada'd given me. There were more than
thirty movies here. Closer to fifty. The ones near the bottom
had notes after them: "Frame 14-1968, bottle on table," and
"Frame 102-166, reference to ale."

I should feed the first twelve in, send them to Mayer to calm him down, but I didn't. I sat on the bed, staring at the list. Next to *Casablanca,* she had written, "Hopeless."

"Hi," Heada said from the door. "It's Tess Trueheart again," and then stood there, looking uncomfortable.

"What is it?" I said, standing up. "Is Mayer back?"

"She's not in 1950," she said, not meeting my eyes. "She's down on Sunset Boulevard. I saw her."

"On Sunset Boulevard?"

"No. On the skids."

Not in a parallel timefeed. Or some never-never-land where people walked through the screen into the movies. Here. On the skids. "Did you talk to her?"

She shook her head. "It was morning rush hour. I was coming back from Mayer's, and I just caught a glimpse of her. You know how rush hour is. I tried to get through the crowd to her, but by the time I made it, she'd gotten off."

"Why would she get off at Sunset Boulevard? Did you see her get off?"

"I told you, I just got a glimpse of her through the crowd. She was lugging all this equipment. But she had to have gotten off at Sunset Boulevard. It was the only station we passed."

"You said she was carrying equipment. What kind of equipment?"

"I don't know. Equipment. I *told* you, I—"

"Just got a glimpse of her. And you're sure it was her?"

She nodded. "I wasn't going to tell you, but Betsy Booth's a tough role to shake. And it's hard to hate Alis, after everything she's done." She gestured at her reflections in the array. "Look at me. Chooch free, klieg free.'' She turned and looked at me. ''I always wanted to be in the movies and now I am.''

She started down the hall again.

''Heada, wait,'' I said, and then was sorry, afraid her face would be full of hope when she turned around, that there would be tears in her eyes.

But this was Heada, who knows everything.

''What's your name?'' I said. ''All I have is your access, and I've never called you anything but Heada.''

She smiled at me knowingly, ruefully. Emma Thompson in *Remains of the Day*. ''I like Heada,'' she said.

Camera whip-pans to medium-shot: LAIT station sign. Diamond screen, "Los Angeles Instransit" in hot pink caps, "Sunset Boulevard" in yellow.

I TOOK THE OPDISK OF ALIS'S ROUTINES AND went down to the skids. There was nobody on them except a huddle of tourates in mouse ears, a very splatted Marilyn, and Elizabeth Taylor, Sidney Poitier, Mary Pickford, Harrison Ford, emerging one by one from ILMGM's golden fog. I watched the signs, waiting for Sunset Boulevard and wondering what Alis was doing there. There was nothing down there but the old freeway.

The Marilyn wove unsteadily over to me. Her white halter dress was stained and splotched, and there was a red smear of lipstick by her ear.

"Want a pop?" she said, looking not at me but at Harrison Ford behind me on the screen.

"No, thanks," I said.

"Okay," she said docilely. "How about you?" She didn't wait for me, or Harrison, to answer. She wandered off and then came back. "Are you a studio exec?" she asked.

"No, sorry," I said.

"I want to be in the movies," she said, and wandered off again.

I kept my eyes fixed on the screen. It went silver for a second between promos, and I caught sight of myself looking clean and responsible and sober. Jimmy Stewart in *Mr. Smith Goes to Washington*. No wonder she'd thought I was a studio exec.

The station sign for Sunset Boulevard came up and I got off. The area hadn't changed. There was still nothing down here, not even lights. The abandoned freeway loomed darkly in the starlight, and I could see a fire a long way off under one of the cloverleafs.

There was no way Alis was here. She must have spotted Heada and gotten off here to keep her from finding out where she was really going. Which was where?

There was another light now, a thin white beam wobbling this way. Ravers, probably, looking for victims. I got back on the skids.

The Marilyn was still there, sitting in the middle of the floor, her legs splayed out, fishing through an open palm full of pills for chooch, illy, klieg. The only equipment a freelancer needs, I thought, which at least means whatever Alis is doing it's not freelancing, and realized I'd been relieved ever since Heada told me about seeing Alis with all that equipment, even though I didn't know where she was. At least she hadn't turned into a freelancer.

It was half past two. Heada had seen Alis at rush hour, which was still four hours away. If Alis went the same place every day. If she hadn't been moving someplace, carrying her luggage. But Heada hadn't said luggage, she'd said equipment. And it couldn't be a comp and monitor because Heada would have recognized those, and anyway, they were light. Heada had said "lugging." What then? A time machine?

The Marilyn had stood up, spilling capsules everywhere, and was heading over the yellow warning strip for the far wall, which was still extolling ILMGM's cavalcade of stars.

"Don't!" I said, and grabbed for her, a foot from the wall.

She looked up at me, her eyes completely dilated. "This is my stop. I have to get off."

"Wrong way, Corrigan," I said, turning her around to face the front. The sign read Beverly Hills, which didn't seem very likely. "Where did you want to get off?"

She shrugged off my arm, and turned back to the screen.

"The way out's that way," I said, pointing to the front.

She shook her head and pointed at Fred Astaire emerging out of the fog. "Through there," she said, and sank down to sitting, her white skirt in a circle. The screen went silver, reflecting her sitting there, fishing through her empty palm, and then to golden fog. The lead-in to the ILMGM promo.

I stared at the wall, which didn't look like a wall, or a mirror. It looked like what it was, a fog of electrons, a veil over emptiness, and for a minute it all seemed possible. For a minute I thought, Alis didn't get off at Sunset Boulevard. She didn't get off the skids at all. She stepped through the screen, like Mia Farrow, like Buster Keaton, and into the past.

I could almost see her in her black skirt and green weskit and gloves, disappearing into the golden fog and emerging on a Hollywood Boulevard full of cars and palm trees and lined with rehearsal halls full of mirrors.

"Anything's Possible," the voice-over roared.

The Marilyn was on her feet again and weaving toward the back wall.

"Not that way," I said, and sprinted after her.

It was a good thing she hadn't been headed for the screens this time—I'd never have made it. By the time I got to her, she was banging on the wall with both fists.

"Let me off!" she shouted. "This is my stop!"

"The way off's this way," I said, trying to turn her, but she must have been doing rave. Her arm was like iron.

"I have to get off here," she said, pounding with the flat of her hands. "Where's the door?"

"The door's that way," I said, wondering if this was how I had been the night Alis brought me home from Burbank. "You can't get off this way."

"She did," she said.

I looked at the back wall and then back at her. "Who did?"

"*She* did," she said. "She went right through the door. I saw her," and puked all over my feet.

MOVIE CLICHE #12: The Moral. A character states the obvious, and everybody gets the point.

SEE: *The Wizard of Oz, Field of Dreams, Love Story, What's New, Pussycat?*

 GOT THE MARILYN OFF AT WILSHIRE AND TOOK her to rehab, by which time she'd pretty much pumped her own stomach, and waited to make sure she checked in.

"Are you sure you've got time to do this?" she said, looking less like Marilyn and more like Jodie Foster in *Taxi Driver*.

"I'm sure." There was plenty of time, now that I knew where Alis was.

While she was filling out paperwork, I accessed Vincent. "I have a question," I said without preamble. "What if you took a frame and substituted an identical frame? Could that get past the fibe-op ID-locks?"

149

"An identical frame? What would be the point of that?"

"Could it?"

"I guess," he said. "Is this for Mayer?"

"Yeah," I said. "What if you substituted a new image that matched the original? Could the ID-locks tell the difference?"

"Matched?"

"A different image that's the same."

"You're splatted," he said, and signed off.

It didn't matter. I already knew the ID-locks couldn't tell the difference. It would take too much memory. And, as Vincent had said, what would be the point of changing an image to one exactly like it?

I waited till the Marilyn was in a bed and getting a ridigaine IV and then got back on the skids. After LaBrea there was nobody on them, but it took me till three-thirty to find the service door to the shut-off section and past five to get it open.

I was worried for a while that Alis had braced it shut, which she had, but not intentionally. One of the fibe-op feed cables was up against it, and when I finally got the door open a crack, all I had to do was push.

She was facing the far wall, looking at the screen that should have been blank in this shut-off section. It wasn't. In the middle of it, Peter Lawford and June Allyson were demonstrating the Varsity Drag to a gymnasium full of college students in party dresses and tuxes. June was wearing a pink dress and pink heels with pompoms, and so was Alis, and their hair was curled under in identical blonde pageboys.

Alis had set the Digimatte on top of its case, with the compositor and pixar beside it on the floor, and snaked the fibe-op cable along the yellow warning strip and around in front of the door to the skids feed. I pushed the cable out from the door, gently, so it wouldn't break the connection, and opened the door far enough so I could see, and then stood, half-hidden by it, and watched her.

"Down on your heels," Peter Lawford instructed, "up on your toes," and went into a triple step. Alis, holding a remote, ff'd past the song and stopped where the dance started, and watched it, her face intent, counting the steps. She rew'd to the end of the song. She punched a button and everyone froze in midstep.

She walked rapidly in the silly high-heeled shoes to the rear of the skids, out of reach of the frame, and pressed a button. Peter Lawford sang, "—that's how it goes."

Alis set the remote down on the floor, her full-skirted dress rustling as she knelt, and then hurried back to her mark and stood, obscuring June Allyson except for one hand and a tail of the pink skirt, waiting for her cue.

It came, Alis went down on her heels, up on her toes, and into a Charleston, with June behind her from this angle like a twin, a shadow. I moved over to where I could see her from the same angle as the Digimatte's processor. June Allyson disappeared, and there was only Alis.

I had expected June Allyson to be wiped from the screen the way Princess Leia had been for the tourates' scene at A Star Is Born, but Alis wasn't making vids for the folks back home, or even trying to project her image on the screen. She was simply rehearsing, and she had only hooked the Digimatte up to feed the fibe-op loop through the processor because that was the way she'd been taught to use it at work. I could see, even from here, that the "record" light wasn't on.

I retreated to the half-open door. She was taller than June Allyson, and her dress was a brighter pink than June's, but the image the Digimatte was feeding back into the fibe-op loop was the corrected version, adjusted for color and focus and lighting. And on some of these routines, practiced for hours and hours in these shut-off sections of the skids, done and redone and done again, that corrected image had been so close to the original that the ID-locks didn't catch it, so close Alis's image had gotten past the guards and onto the fibe-op source. And Alis had managed the impossible.

She flubbed a turn, stopped, clattered over to the remote in her pompomed heels, rew'd to the middle section just before the flub, and froze it. She glanced at the Digimatte's clock and then punched a button and hurried back to her mark.

She only had another half hour, if that, and then she would have to dismantle this equipment and take it back to Hollywood Boulevard, set it up, open up shop. I should let her. I could show her the opdisk another time, and I had found out what I wanted to know. I should shut the door and leave her to rehearse. But I didn't. I leaned against the door, and stood there, watching her dance.

She went through the middle section three more times, working the clumsiness out of the turn, and then rew'd to the end of the song and went through the whole thing. Her face was intent, alert, the way it had been that night watching the Continental, but it lacked the delight, the rapt, abandoned quality of the Beguine.

I wondered if it was because she was still learning the routine, or if she would ever have it. The smile June Allyson turned on Peter Lawford was pleased, not joyful, and the "Varsity Drag" number itself was only so-so. Hardly Cole Porter.

It came to me then, watching her patiently go over the same steps again and again, as Fred must have done, all alone in a rehearsal hall before the movie had even begun filming, that I had been wrong about her.

I had thought that she believed, like Ruby Keeler and ILMGM, that anything was possible. I had tried to tell her it wasn't, that just because you want something doesn't mean you can have it. But she had already known that, long before I met her, long before she came to Hollywood. Fred Astaire had died the year she was born, and she could never, never, never, in spite of VR and computer graphics and copyrights, dance the Beguine with him.

And all this, the costumes and the classes and the rehearsing, were simply a substitute, something to do instead. Like fighting in the Resistance. Compared to the impossibility of what Alis was unfortunate enough to want, breaking into a Hollywood populated by puppets and pimps must have seemed a snap.

Peter Lawford took June Allyson's hand, and Alis misjudged the turn and crashed into empty air. She picked up the remote to rew, glanced toward the station sign, and saw me. She stood looking at me for a long moment, and then walked over and shut off the Digimatte.

"Don't—" I said.

"Don't what?" she said, unhooking connections. She shrugged a white lab coat on over the pink dress. "Don't waste your time trying to find a dancing teacher because there aren't any?" She buttoned up the coat and went over to the input and disconnected the feed. "As you can see, I've already figured that out. Nobody in Hollywood knows how to dance. Or if they do, they're splatted on chooch, trying to forget." She began looping the feed into a coil. "Are you?"

She glanced up at the station sign and then laid the coiled feed on top of the Digimatte and knelt next to the compositor, skirt rustling. "Because if you are, I don't have time to take you home and keep you from falling off the skids and fend off your advances. I have to get this stuff back." She slid the pixar into its case and snapped it shut.

"I'm not splatted," I said. "And I'm not drunk. I've been looking for you for six weeks."

She lifted the Digimatte down and into its case and began stowing wires. "Why? So you can convince me I'm not Ruby Keeler? That the musical's dead and anything I can do, comps can do better? Fine. I'm convinced."

She sat down on the case and unbuckled the pompomed heels. "You win," she said. "I can't dance in the movies." She looked over at the mirrored wall, shoe in hand. "It's impossible."

"No," I said. "I didn't come to tell you that."

She stuck the heels in one of the pockets of the lab coat.

"Then what did you come to tell me? That you want your list of accesses back? Fine." She slid her feet into a pair of slip-ons and stood up. "I've learned just about all the chorus numbers and solos anyway, and this isn't going to work for partnered dancing. I'm going to have to find something else."

"I don't want the accesses back," I said.

She pulled off the blond pageboy and shook out her beautiful backlit hair. "Then what do you want?"

You, I thought. I want you.

She stood up abruptly and jammed the wig in her other pocket. "Whatever it is, it'll have to wait." She slung the coil of feed over her shoulder. "I've got a job to go to." She bent to pick up the cases.

"Let me help you," I said, starting toward her.

"No, thanks," she said, shouldering the pixar and hoisting the Digimatte. "I can do it myself."

"Then I'll hold the door for you," I said, and opened it.

She pushed through.

Rush hour. Packed mirror to mirror with Ray Milland and Rosalind Russell on their way to work, none of whom turned to look at Alis. They were all looking at the walls, which were going full blast: ILMGM, More Copyrights Than There Are in Heaven. A promo for *Beverly Hills Cop 15,* a promo for a remake of *The Three Musketeers.*

I pulled the door shut behind me, and a River Phoenix, squatting on the yellow warning strip, looked up from a razor blade and a palmful of powder, but he was too splatted to register what he was seeing. His eyes didn't even focus.

Alis was already halfway to the front of the skids, her eyes on the station sign. It blinked "Hollywood Boulevard," and she pushed her way toward the exit, with me following in her wake, and out onto the Boulevard.

It was still as dark as it gets, but everything was open. And there were still (or maybe already) tourates around. Two old guys in Bermuda shorts and vidcams were at the Happily Ever After booth, watching Ryan O'Neal save Ali MacGraw's life.

Alis stopped at the grille of A Star Is Born and fumbled with her key, trying to insert the card without putting any of her stuff down. The two tourates wandered over.

"Here," I said, taking the key. I opened the gate and took the Digimatte from her.

"Do you have Charles Bronson?" one of the oldates said.

"We're not open yet," I said. "I have something I have to show you," I said to Alis.

"What? The latest puppet show? An automatic rehearsal program?" She started setting up the Digimatte, plugging in the cables and fibe-op feed, shoving the Digimatte into position.

"I always wanted to be in *Death Wish,*" the oldate said. "Do you have that?"

"We're not *open,*" I said.

"Here's the menu," Alis said, switching it on for the oldate. "We don't have Charles Bronson, but we have got a scene from *The Magnificent Seven.*" She pointed to it.

"You have to see this, Alis," I said, and shoved in the opdisk, glad I'd preset it and didn't have to call anything up. *On the Town* came up on the screen.

"I have customers to—" Alis said, and stopped.

I had set the disk to "Next, please" after fifteen seconds. *On the Town* disappeared, and *Singin' in the Rain* came up.

Alis turned angrily to me. "Why did you—"

"I didn't," I said. "You did." I pointed at the screen. *Tea for Two* came up, and Alis, in red curls, Charlestoned her way toward the front of the screen.

"It's not a paste-up," I said. "Look at them. They're the movies you've been rehearsing, aren't they? Aren't they?"

On the screen Alis was high-stepping with her blue parasol.

"You talked about *Singin' in the Rain* that night I met you. And I could have guessed some of the others. They're all full-length shot and continuous take." I pointed at her in her blue bustle. "But I didn't even know what movie that was from."

Hats Off came up. "And I'd never seen some of these."

"I didn't—" she said, looking at the screen.

"The Digimatte does a superimpose on the fibe-op image coming in and puts it on disk," I said, showing her. "That image goes back through the loop, too, and the fibe-op source randomly checks the pattern of pixels and automatically rejects any image that's been changed. Only you weren't trying to change the image. You were trying to duplicate it. And you succeeded. You matched the moves perfectly, so perfectly the Brownian check thought it was the same image, so perfectly it didn't reject it, and the image made it onto the fibe-op source." I waved my hand at the screen, where she was dancing to "42nd Street."

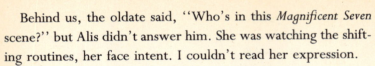
Behind us, the oldate said, "Who's in this *Magnificent Seven* scene?" but Alis didn't answer him. She was watching the shifting routines, her face intent. I couldn't read her expression.

"How many are there?" she said, still looking at the screen.

"I've found fourteen," I said. "You rehearsed more than that, right? The ones that got past the ID-locks are almost all dancers with the same shape of face and features you have. Did you do any Ann Millers?"

"*Kiss Me Kate*," she said.

"I thought you might have," I said. "Her face is too round. Your features wouldn't match closely enough to get past the ID-lock. It only works where there's already a resemblance." I pointed at the screen. "There are two others I found that aren't on the disk because they're in litigation. *White Christmas* and *Seven Brides for Seven Brothers*."

She turned to look at me. "*Seven Brides?* Are you sure?"

"You're right there in the barnraising scene," I said. "Why?"

She had turned back to the screen, frowning at Shirley Temple, who was dancing with Alis and Jack Haley in military uniforms. "Maybe—" she said to herself.

"I told you dancing in the movies was impossible," I said. "I was wrong. There you are."

As I said it, the screen went blank, and the oldate said loudly, "How about that guy who says, 'Make my day!' Do you have him?"

I reached to start the disk again, but Alis had already turned away.

"I'm afraid we don't have Clint Eastwood either. The scene from *Magnificent Seven* has Steve McQueen and Yul Brynner," she said. "Would you like to see it?" and busied herself punching in the access.

"Does he have to shave his head?" his friend said.

"No," Alis said, reaching for a black shirt and pants, a black hat. "The Digimatte takes care of that." She started setting up the tape equipment, showing the oldate where to stand and what to do, oblivious of his friend, who was still talking about Charles Bronson, oblivious of me.

Well, what had I expected? That she'd be overjoyed to see herself up there, that she'd fling her arms around me like Natalie Wood in *The Searchers*? I hadn't done anything. Except tell her she'd accomplished something she hadn't been trying to do, something she'd turned down standing on this very boulevard.

"Yul *Brynner*," the oldate's friend said disgustedly, "and no Charles Bronson."

On the Town was on the screen again. Alis switched it off without a glance and called up *The Magnificent Seven*.

"You want Charles Bronson and they give you Steve Mc-Queen," the oldate grumbled. "They always make you settle for second best."

That's what I love about the movies. There's always some minor character standing around to tell you the moral, just in case you're too dumb to figure it out for yourself.

"You never get what you want," the oldate said.

"Yeah," I said. " 'There's no place like home,' " and headed for the skids.

VERA MILES: [*Running out to corral, where RANDOLPH SCOTT is saddling horse*] You were going to leave, just like that? Without even saying good-bye?

RANDOLPH SCOTT: [*Cinching girth on horse*] I got a score to settle. And you got a young man to tend to. I got the bullet out of that arm of his, but it needs bandaging. [*RANDOLPH SCOTT steps in stirrup and swings up on horse*]

VERA MILES: Will I see you again? How will I know you're all right?

RANDOLPH SCOTT: I reckon I'll be all right. [*Tips hat*] You take care, ma'am. [*Wheels horse around and rides off into sunset*]

VERA MILES: [*Calling after him*] I'll never forget what you've done for me! Never!

I WENT HOME AND STARTED WORK. I DID THE ones that mattered first—restoring the double cigarette-lighting in *Now, Voyager,* putting the uranium back in the wine bottle in *Notorious,* reinebriating Lee Marvin's horse in *Cat Ballou.* And the ones I liked: *Ninotchka* and *Rio Bravo* and *Double Indemnity.* And *Brides,* which came out of litigation the day after I saw Alis. It was beeping at me when I woke up. I put Howard Keel's drink and whiskey bottle back in the opening scene, and then ff'd to the barnraising and turned the pan of corn bread back into a jug before I watched Alis.

It was too bad I couldn't have shown it to her, she'd seemed so surprised the number had made it onto film. She must have had trouble with it, and no wonder. All those lifts and no partner—I wondered what equipment she'd had to lug down Hollywood Boulevard and onto the skids to make it look like she was in the air. It would have been nice if she could see how happy she looked doing those lifts.

I put the barnraising dance on the disk with the others, in case Russ Tamblyn's estate or Warner appealed, and then erased all my transaction records, in case Mayer yanked the Cray.

I figured I had two weeks, maybe three if the Columbia take-over really went through. Mayer'd be so busy trying to make up his mind which way to jump he wouldn't have time to worry about AS's, and neither would Arthurton. I thought about call-ing Heada—she'd know what was happening—and then de-cided that was probably a bad idea. Anyway, she was probably busy scrambling to keep her job.

A week anyway. Enough time to give Myrna Loy back her hangover and watch the rest of the musicals. I'd already found most of them, except for *Good News* and *The Birds and the Bees.* I put the *dulce la leche* back in *Guys and Dolls* while I was at it, and the brandy back in *My Fair Lady* and made Frank Morgan in *Summer Holiday* back into a drunk. It went slower than I wanted it to, and after a week and a half, I stopped and put everything Alis had done on disk *and* tape, expecting Mayer to knock on the door any minute, and started in on *Casablanca.*

There was a knock on the door. I ff'd to the end where Rick's bar was still full of lemonade, took the disk of Alis's dancing and stuck it down the side of my shoe, and opened the door.

It was Alis.

The hall behind her was dark, but her hair, pulled into a bun, caught the light from somewhere. She looked tired, like she had just come from practicing. She still had on her lab coat. I could see white stockings and Mary Janes below it, and an inch or so of pink ruffle. I wondered what she'd been doing—the "Abba-Dabba Honeymoon" number from *Two Weeks with Love*? Or something from *By the Light of the Silvery Moon*?

She reached in the pocket of the lab coat and held out the opdisk I'd given her. "I came to bring this back to you."

"Keep it," I said.

She looked at it a minute, and then stuck it in her pocket. "Thanks," she said, and pulled it out again. "I'm surprised so many of the routines made it on. I wasn't very good when I started," she said, turning it over. "I'm still not very good."

"You're as good as Ruby Keeler," I said.

She grinned. "She was somebody's girlfriend."

"You're as good as Vera-Ellen. And Debbie Reynolds. And Virginia Gibson."

She frowned, and looked at the disk again and then at me, as if trying to decide whether to tell me something. "Heada told me about her job," she said, and that wasn't it. "Location assistant. That's great." She looked over at the array, where Bogart was toasting Ingrid. "She said you were putting the movies back the way they were."

"Not all the movies," I said, pointing at the disk in her hand. "Some remakes are better than the original."

"Won't you get fired?" she said. "Putting the AS's back in, I mean?"

"Almost certainly," I said. "But it is a fah, fah bettah thing I do than I have evah done before. It is a——"

"*Tale of Two Cities,* Ronald Colman," she said, looking at the screens where Bogart was saying good-bye to Ingrid, at the disk, at the screens again, trying to work up to what she had to say.

I said it for her. "You're leaving."

She nodded, still not looking at me.

"Where are you going? Back to River City?"

"That's from *The Music Man,*" she said, but she didn't smile. "I can't go any farther by myself. I need somebody to teach me the heel-and-toe work Eleanor Powell does. And I need a partner."

Just for a moment, no, not even a moment, the flicker of a frame, I thought about what might have been if I hadn't spent those long splatted semesters dismantling highballs, if I had spent them out in Burbank instead, practicing kick-turns.

"After what you said the other night, I thought I might be able to use a positioning armature and a data harness for the lifts, and I tried it. It worked, I guess. I mean, it—"

Her voice cut off awkwardly like she'd intended to say something more, and I wondered what it was, and what it was I'd said to her. That Fred might be coming out of litigation?

"But the balance isn't the same as a real person," she said. "And I need experience learning routines, not just copying them off the screen."

So she was going someplace where they were still doing liveactions. "Where?" I said. "Buenos Aires?"

"No," she said. "China."

China.

"They're doing ten liveactions a year," she said.

And twenty purges. Not to mention provincial uprisings. And antiforeigner riots.

"Their liveactions aren't very good. They're terrible, actually. Most of them are propaganda films and martial-arts things, but a couple of them last year were musicals." She smiled ruefully. "They like Gene Kelly."

Gene Kelly. But it would be real routines. And a man's arm around her waist instead of a data harness, a man's hands lifting her. The real thing.

"I leave tomorrow morning," she said. "I was packing, and I found the disk and thought maybe you wanted it back."

"No," I said, and then, so I wouldn't have to tell her good-bye, "Where are you flying out of?"

"San Francisco," she said. "I'm taking the skids up tonight. And I'm still not packed." She looked at me, waiting for me to say my line.

And I had plenty to choose from. If there's anything the movies are good at, it's good-byes. From "Be careful, darling!" to "Don't let's ask for the moon when we have the stars," to "Come back, Shane!" Even, "*Hasta la vista,* baby."

But I didn't say them. I stood there and looked at her, with her beautiful, backlit hair and her unforgettable face. At what I wanted and couldn't have, not even for a few minutes.

And what if I said "Stay"? What if I promised to find her a teacher, get her a part, put on a show? Right. With a Cray that had maybe ten minutes of memory, a Cray I wouldn't have as soon as Mayer found out what I'd been doing?

Behind me on the screen, Bogart was saying, "There's no

place for you here,'' and looking at Ingrid, trying to make the moment last forever. In the background, the plane's propellers were starting to turn, and in a minute the Nazis would show up.

They stood there, looking at each other, and tears welled up in Ingrid's eyes, and Vincent could mess with his tears program forever and never get it right. Or maybe he would. They had made *Casablanca* out of dry ice and cardboard. And it was the real thing.

''I have to go,'' Alis said.

''I know,'' I said, and smiled at her. ''We'll always have Paris.''

And according to the script, she was supposed to give me one last longing look and get on the plane with Paul Henreid, and why is it I still haven't learned that Heada is always right?

''Good-bye,'' Alis said, and then she was in my arms, and I was kissing her, kissing her, and she was unbuttoning the lab coat, taking down her hair, unbuttoning the pink gingham dress, and some part of me was thinking, ''This is important,'' but she had the dress off, and the pantaloons, and I had her on the bed, and she didn't fade, she didn't morph into Heada, I was on her and in her, and we were moving together, easily, effortlessly, our outstretched hands almost but not quite touching on the tangled sheets.

I kept my gaze on her hands, flexing and stretching in passion, knowing if I looked at her face it would be freeze-framed on my brain forever, klieg or no klieg, afraid if I did she might be looking at me kindly, or, worse, not be looking at me at all. Looking through me, past me, at two dancers on a starry floor.

"Tom!" she said, coming, and I looked down at her. Her hair was spread out on the pillow, backlit and beautiful, and her face was intent, the way it had been that night at the party, watching Fred and Ginge on the freescreen, rapt and beautiful and sad. And focused, finally, on me.

MOVIE CLICHE #1: The Happy Ending. Self-explanatory.

SEE: *An Officer and a Gentleman, An Affair to Remember, Sleepless in Seattle, The Miracle of Morgan's Creek, Shall We Dance, Great Expectations.*

*I*T'S BEEN THREE YEARS, DURING WHICH TIME China has gone through four provincial uprisings and six student riots, and Mayer has gone through three takeovers and eight bosses, the next to last of whom moved him up to Executive Vice-President.

Mayer didn't tumble to my putting the AS's back in for nearly three months, by which time I'd finished the whole *Thin Man* series, *The Maltese Falcon,* and all the Westerns, and Arthurton was on his way out.

Heada, still costarring as Joan Blondell, talked Mayer out of killing me and into making a stirring speech about Censorship and Deep Love for the Movies and getting himself spectacularly fired just in time for the new boss to hire him back as "the only moral person in this whole poppated town."

Heada got promoted to set director and then (that next-to-last boss) to Assistant Producer in Charge of New Projects, and promptly hired me to direct a remake. Happy endings all around.

In the meantime, I programmed happy endings for Happily Ever After and graduated and looked for Alis. I found her in *Pennies from Heaven,* and in *Into the Woods,* the last musical ever made, and in *Small Town Girl.* I thought I'd found them all. Until tonight.

I watched the scene in the Indy again, looking at the silver tap shoes and the platinum wig and thinking about musicals. *Indiana Jones and the Temple of Doom* isn't one. "Anything Goes" is the only number in it, and it's only there because one of the scenes takes place in a nightclub, and they're the floor show.

And maybe that's the way to go. The remake I'm working on isn't a musical either—it's a weeper about a couple of star-crossed lovers—but I could change the hotel dining room scene into a nightclub. And then, the boss after next, do a remake with a nightclub setting, and put Fred (who's bound to be out of litigation by then) in it, just in one featured number. That was all he was in *Flying Down to Rio,* a featured number, thirtyish, slightly balding, who could dance a little. And look what happened.

And before you know it, Mayer will be telling everybody the musical's coming back, and I'll get assigned the remake of *42nd Street* and find out where Alis is and book the skids and we'll put on a show. Anything's possible.

Even time travel.

I accessed Vincent the other day to borrow his edit program, and he told me time travel's a bust. "We were *this* close," he said, his thumb and forefinger almost touching. "Theoretically, the Casimir effect should work for time as well as space, but they've sent image after image into a negative-matter region, and nothing. No overlap at all. I guess maybe there are some things that just aren't possible."

He's wrong. The night Alis left, she said, "After what you said the other night, I thought maybe I could use a data harness for the lifts," and I had wondered what it was I'd said, and when I showed her the opdisk, she'd said, "*Seven Brides for Seven Brothers?* Are you sure?"

"It's not on the disk," I'd said, "it's in litigation," and it had stayed in litigation till the next day. And when I checked, it had been in litigation the whole time I looked for her.

And for eight months before that, in a National Treasure suit the Film Preservation Society had brought. The night I saw *Brides,* it had been out of litigation exactly two hours. And had gone back in an hour later.

Alis had only been working at A Star Is Born for six months. *Brides* had been in litigation the whole time. Until after I found her. Until after I told her I'd seen her in it. And when I told her, she'd said, "*Seven Brides for Seven Brothers? Are you sure?*" and I'd thought she was surprised because the jumps and lifts were so hard, surprised because she hadn't been trying to superimpose her image on the screen.

Brides hadn't come out of litigation till the next day.

And a week and a half later Alis came to me. She came straight from the skids, straight from practicing with the harness and the armature that she'd thought might work, "after what you said the other night." And it had worked. "—I guess," she'd said. "I mean—"

She'd come straight from practice, wearing Virginia Gibson's pink gingham dress, Virginia Gibson's pantaloons, wearing her costume for the barnraising dance she'd just done. The barnraising dance I'd seen her in six weeks before she ever did it. And my theory about her having somehow gone back in time was right after all, even if it was only her image, only pixels on a screen. She hadn't been trying to discover time travel either. She had only been trying to learn routines, but the screen she'd been rehearsing in front of wasn't a screen. It was a negative-matter region, full of randomized electrons and potential overlaps. Full of possibilities.

Nothing's impossible, Vincent, I think, watching Alis do kick-turns in her sequined leotard. Not if you know what you want.

Heada is accessing me. "I was wrong. The Ford Tri-Motor's at the beginning of the second one. *Indiana Jones and the Temple of Doom.* Beginning with frame—"

"I found it," I say, frowning at the screen where Alis, in her platinum wig, is doing a brush step.

"What's wrong?" Heada says. "Isn't it going to work?"

"I'm not sure," I say. "When's the Fred Astaire suit going to be settled?"

"A month," she says promptly. "But it's going right back in. Sofracima-Rizzoli's claiming copyright infringement."

"Who the hell is Sofracima-Rizzoli?"

"The studio that owns the rights to a movie Fred Astaire made in the seventies. *The Purple Taxi*. I figure they'll settle. Three months. Why?" she says suspiciously.

"The plane in *Flying Down to Rio*. I've decided that's what I want."

"A biplane? You don't have to wait for that. There are tons of other movies with biplanes in them. *The Blue Max, Wings, High Road to China*—" She stops, looking unhappy.

"Do they have skids in China?" I say.

"Are you kidding? They're lucky to have bicycles. And enough to eat. Why?" she says, suddenly interested. "Have you found out where Alis is?"

"No."

Heada hesitates, trying to decide whether to tell me something. "The assistant set director's back from China. He says the word is, it's Cultural Revolution 3. Book burnings, re-education, they've shut at least one studio down and arrested the whole film crew."

I should be worried, but I'm not, and Heada, who knows everything, pounces immediately.

"Is she back?" she says, "Have you had word from her?"

"No," I say, because I have finally learned how to lie to Heada, and because it's true. I don't know where she is, and I haven't had word from her. But I've gotten a message.

Fred Astaire has been out of litigation twice since Alis left, once between copyright suits for exactly eight seconds, the other time last month when the AFI filed an injunction claiming he was a historic landmark.

That time I was ready. I had the Beguine number on opdisk, backup, and tape, and was ready to check it before the watch-and-warn had even stopped beeping.

It was the middle of the night, as usual, and at first I thought I was still asleep or having one last flash.

"Enhance upper left," I said, and watched it again. And again. And the next morning.

It looked the same every time, and the message was loud and clear: Alis is all right, in spite of uprisings and revolutions, and she's found a place to practice and somebody to teach her Eleanor Powell's heel-and-toe steps. And she's going to come back, because China doesn't have skids, and when she does, she's going to dance the Beguine with Fred Astaire.

Or maybe she already has. I saw her in the barnraising number in *Brides* six weeks before she did it, and it's been four since I saw her in *Melody*. Maybe she's already back. Maybe she's already done it.

I don't think so. I've promised the current A Star Is Born James Dean a lifetime supply of chooch to tell me if anybody touches the Digimatte, and Fred's still in litigation. And I don't know how far back in time the overlap goes. Six weeks before she did it was only when I *saw* her in *Brides*. There's no telling how long before that her image was there. Under two years, because it wasn't in *42nd Street* when I watched it the first time, when I was first starting Mayer's list, and yeah, I know I was

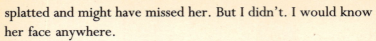

splatted and might have missed her. But I didn't. I would know her face anywhere.

So under two years. And Heada, who knows everything, says Fred will be out of litigation in three months.

In the meantime, I keep busy, doing remakes and trying to make them good, getting Mayer to talk ILMGM into copyrighting Ruby Keeler and Eleanor Powell, working for the Resistance. I have even come up with a happy ending for *Casablanca.*

It is after the war, and Rick has come back to Casablanca after fighting with the Resistance, after who knows what hardships. The Café Américain has burned down, and everybody's gone, even the parrot, even Sam, and Bogie stands and looks at the rubble for a long time, and then starts picking through the mess, trying to see what he can salvage.

He finds the piano, but when he tips it upright, half the keys fall out. He fishes an unbroken bottle of scotch out of the rubble and sets it on the piano and starts looking around for a glass. And there she is, standing in what's left of the doorway.

She looks different, her hair's pulled back, and she looks thinner, tired. You can see by looking at her that Paul Henreid's dead and she's gone through a lot, but you'd know that face anywhere.

She stands there in the door, and Bogie, still trying to find a glass, looks up and sees her.

No dialogue. No music. No clinch, in spite of Heada's benighted ideas. Just the two of them, who never thought they'd see each other again, standing there looking at each other.

When I'm done with my remake, I'll put my *Casablanca* ending in Happily Ever After's comp for the tourates.

In the meantime, I have to separate my star-crossed lovers and send them off to suffer assorted hardships and pay for their sins. For which I need a plane.

I put the "Anything Goes" number on disk and backup, in case Kate Capshaw goes into litigation, and then ff to the Ford Tri-Motor and save that, too, in case the biplane doesn't work.

"*High Road to China*," I say, and then cancel it before it has a chance to come up. "Simultaneous display. Screen one, *Temple of Doom*. Two, *Singin' in the Rain*. Three, *Good News* . . ."

I go through the litany, and Alis appears on the screens, one after the other, in tap pants and bustles and green weskits, ponytails and red curls and shingled bobs. Her face looks the same in all of them, intent, alert, concentrating on the steps and the music, unaware that she is conquering encryptions and Brownian checks and time.

"Screen Eighteen," I say, "*Seven Brides for Seven Brothers*," and she twirls across the floor and leaps into the arms of Russ Tamblyn. And he has conquered time, too. They all have, Gene and Ruby and Fred, in spite of the death of the musical, in spite of the studio execs and the hackates and the courts, conquering time in a turn, a smile, a lift, capturing for a permanent moment what we want and can't have.

I have been working on weepers too long. I need to get on with the business at hand, pick a plane, save the sentiment for my lovers' Big Farewell.

"Cancel, all screens," I say, "Center screen, *High Road to*—" and then stop and stare at the silver screen, like Ray Milland craving a drink in *The Lost Weekend*.

"Center screen," I say. "Frame 96-1100. No sound. *Broad-way Melody of 1940*," and sit down on the bed.

They are tapping side by side, dressed in white, lost in the music I cannot hear and the time steps that took them weeks to practice, dancing easily, without effort. Her light brown hair catches the light from somewhere.

Alis swings into a turn, her white skirt swirling out in the same clear arc as Eleanor's—check and Brownian check—and that must have taken weeks, too.

Next to her, casual, elegant, oblivious to copyrights and take-overs, Fred taps out a counterpoint ripple, and Alis answers it back, and turns to smile over her shoulder.

"Freeze," I say, and she stops, still turning, her hand out-stretched and almost touching mine.

I lean forward, looking at the face I have seen ever since that first night watching her from the door, that face I would know anywhere. We'll always have Paris.

"Forward three frames and hold," I say, and she flashes me a delighted, an infinitely promising, smile.

"Forward realtime," I say, and there is Alis, as she should be, dancing in the movies.

THE END

Roll credits

About the Author

CONNIE WILLIS has received six Nebula Awards and five Hugo Awards for her fiction, and the John W. Campbell Award for her first novel, *Lincoln's Dreams*. Her first short story collection, *Fire Watch*, was a *New York Times* Notable Book, and her latest novel, *Doomsday Book*, won the Nebula and Hugo Awards. She is also the author of *Impossible Things*, a short story collection, and *Uncharted Territory*. Ms. Willis lives in Greeley, Colorado, with her family.